Historical Fiction / Art World 1964-1980

FLAME

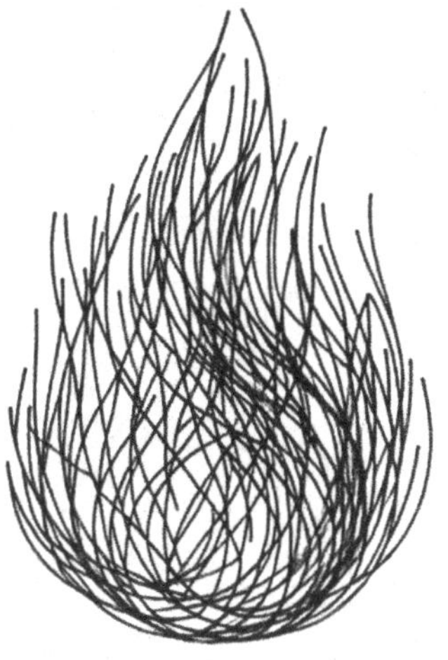

Roland James Ballard

FLAME

James Ballard writing as Roland James Ballard

First Edition 2024

ISBN 13: 978-1-952685-81-1

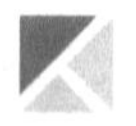

Kitsap Publishing
Poulsbo, WA•USA

Introduction

SoHo is a signature place, and 1964 through 1980 is a significant period in the history of Modern Art and our culture.

Many of the characters and descriptions in the story are based on my experience as an artist living and exhibiting art in *SoHo* during my formative years.

Qwerty Blanc, Nomo, and Gunther Reinhardt are purely fictional characters who may resemble real people, but are figments of my imagination.

Time and seasons have passed, and the SoHo described herein no longer exists, although the iconic cast-iron buildings remain.

A few of the original artists and loft residents can still be found on the quiet streets of what once was SoHo in its glorious heyday.

Travel back to those glory days through the eyes of Qwerty Blanc and his story.

Jim

Chapter One

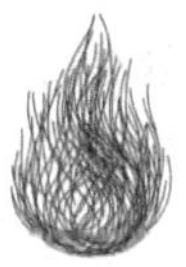

Andy

The air was thick with a mix of scents and traces of past scenes. A cigarette burned slowly in the corner, sending wisps of smoke swirling upward. The ember turned to ash, falling gently onto the uneven wooden floor of the loft. Qwerty watched as the particles of ash floated down as if weightless, suspended on beams of light that pierced through the space. He found himself captivated by this moment as his eyes scanned the scene. The moment held a special kind of magic. It was as though there was an unspoken code of conduct here, codes of cool that he was desperately trying to get right. This loft, known as the Factory near Union Square in New York City 1972, was home to Andy Warhol, and today, it opened its doors to him. Andy's camera captured the atmospheric light, while his eye and mind captured the subject.

Qwerty was tall, lean, and handsome. His long brown hair turned blond in the summer sun, and his eyes were the color of the sky on a clear afternoon.

Qwerty laid back on the mattress, shirtless and clueless about what he was doing there. Andy picked his head up from behind the camera and asked, "How does it feel to be a star in the art world?"

Qwerty thought that was a funny question coming from an art world icon. He had no idea why anyone cared about him or his role in the art world. Ten years ago, artists from a movement in art that didn't have an official name, much less any agreement on what the group stood for, accepted him into what eventually became known as Fluxus. They agreed that there were no rules or special qualifications to make art and were bound together in their search for something new. The methods of creating art crossed all disciplines and materials. Qwerty's approach to creating art matched perfectly. His art was about fire, and it was currently on fire in the art market. Although he had no formal art education, he intuitively understood modern art. He also found a sense of community in the downtown New York neighborhood that was becoming known as SoHo.

"Andy, I have a question for you. Why do artists find it so difficult to talk to each other about their work?"

"Everyone is afraid of the darkness when the lights go out. Artists aren't afraid because they know that nothing changes when the lights go back on. They are afraid of only one thing: who turned off the lights. They know it wasn't them."

Qwerty had only imagined that Andy said that. Andy's actual response was, "That's easy. Art is not about talking. Other people talk about art. Artists do the art."

A plump little man with drooping eyelids sat curled up in a ball in the corner. His skin slid over his body like the pasty glue used in elementary schools for papier mache. He was a regular at the Factory and downtown New York clubs like Max's Kansas City, a nightclub frequented by Lou Reed and Andy's regular followers. People referred to him as Taylor. It wasn't easy to understand why Taylor was a regular at the Factory. His face resembled the portrait of Benjamin Franklin on the one-hundred-dollar bill. Despite the apparent drawbacks in his appearance, Taylor had a kinky charm and vulnerability that drew people in.

"Since your work is all about fire, tie me to a barbecue spit and pretend to roast me for your next piece," Taylor said to Qwerty.

"That is an interesting idea, Taylor. The title could be Eat Me," Andy added.

After a few moments, Qwerty said, " Where are you from, Andy?"

Taylor replied, "He is from Mars."

Andy said, "Pittsburgh."

"Pittsburgh? I wonder if anyone is actually born in New York City. I was born in upstate New York." Qwerty said with a smile.

Qwerty was in awe of Andy and the characters that inhabited his world. Andy's fame went beyond the art world. He was taking his success to a higher level. Qwerty was content to observe and admire the energy and work ethic that most people didn't see firsthand. Andy had gained access to the elusive ruling class of the art and financial world. The question became how much exposure to this elite group they would tolerate. The New York social order allowed artists into their circle. The collecting of work and socializing with artists was a symbol to others that they were culturally elite. Being a subject in Andy's collection of portraits was especially in vogue. Andy took full advantage of their egos and desire to be identified with art.

The photoshoot was wrapped up, and Andy suggested they go to lunch. Fortunately, Taylor was too stoned to move and stayed behind. As they crossed the open loft of the Factory, there were groups of people chatting and moving about. There were also art projects on the floor and walls. The large areas of white paper and canvases were filled with glorious color and energy. Qwerty was in awe of the amount of work in progress. It was no surprise that Andy preferred to use the freight elevator. Most visitors and tenants in the building used the passenger elevator, but for Andy, the freight elevator was a reminder that the Factory was all about working.

The freight elevator moaned and creaked its way to the loft, and the noisy gate opened to let them in. Upon entering the elevator, Qwerty whistled a tune, indicating that they had stepped into what he considered a birdcage. The elevator, with its cables and weights, indeed resembled a suspended birdcage. The elevator operator's name was Izzy. He chewed on an old cigar that, apparently, he lit once or twice a day. He had a tattooed number on his forearm and was likely a survivor of the Holocaust. Izzy seemed cheerful but unimpressed with anyone or anything they had to say. There were characters in New York City of the post-World War II period that were part of the fabric of everyday life. No one seemed to know who they were or where they came from. These people were essential to the equipment they operated or the products they sold. Some of these characters, like Izzy, emigrated from Europe after the Nazi occupation, and there were a variety of other workers that came from Puerto Rico. They all enriched the fabric of the big city culture and they all fascinated Qwerty.

When they reached the street lobby, Izzy pulled back the gate, took out his cigar and spit on the floor. It was an unceremonious exit from the famous Factory building.

Entering the bright light of the street from the freight entrance was jarring, and Qwerty became immersed in the sights and sounds of the city. The intimacy of the studio was replaced by the array of colors and ambient noise of cars and trucks. Everything seemed in motion, as did all the streets in New York City. As they walked down Mercer Street on their way to a lunch spot just off West 4th Street, they had to jump out of the way of an avalanche of cardboard tubes that rolled off the back of a truck unloading on the sidewalk. Trucks were loading and unloading bales of material fabrics and trimmings leftover from the Garment Center, now bound for somewhere in the Spanish-speaking South. The material would find an unintended new purpose. In some building lofts, the leftovers were being stitched together for small market outlets of their own. At this time, the area and other areas near the neighborhood known as SoHo were nearing the end of transition. The buildings transitioned from a collection of small-scale sweatshops and recycling lofts to an area where young artists filled the lofts with their dreams and artwork. The combination of cheap grand space and the isolation created by the closing businesses was irresistible. Andy commented that artists were tricksters who always seemed to find the resources for unusual and grand studio spaces even if they didn't have money.

Andy opened the door to the corner storefront. This restaurant represented the new wave of eating that catered to artists. The interior was rustic, lofty, and known for great healthy lunches. Ten years prior to that, lunch in SoHo was catered to business owners, and one of the favorites was the dairy cafeteria. There were reminders of the Pale with Borscht and Kasha Vanishkes, as well as a bonus of a free seltzer. The atmosphere in the cafeteria was loud and busy; there were tables and a counter that served sandwiches. Street stands along the buildings offered cuchifritos for workers and knishes for various shop and building owners. There were basically two food choices in SoHo before the artists moved in. One was Yiddish; the other was Spanish. At this time, food establishments transitioned to serve artists and art collectors who were spending Thursday nights and Saturdays in the new galleries, which followed the artists to SoHo. The restaurant that Andy chose was simply called Food.

Robert Rauschenberg sat at a booth near the entry with his studio assistant, Hisachika Takahashi and his manager-curator David White. Artists were not only pushing back on American culture but also challenging tastes in cooking. Robert was passionate about cooking. Sachika took over the cooking at his studio and was a big supporter of the restaurant Food.

Robert and Andy, along with Jasper Johns, James Rosenquist, and Roy Lichtenstein, were the anchor Pop Artists of the Leo Castelli Gallery. At this time, Robert Rauschenberg was the gold standard in the art world. His paintings, prints, and assemblages were well respected and commanded top prices in the market. The younger artists considered his work part of the establishment. There was a disconnect between established art and art that the next generation of artists was creating in the studios of SoHo.

Robert was leaving, but he stopped at their table to greet Andy. Robert's face was pleasant and inviting and seemed to have permanent smile wrinkles. Andy and Robert appeared to be quite fond of each other. Qwerty remembered seeing them posing together next to one of Robert's sculptures at the Castelli Gallery. It was a stuffed goat with an old tire around its neck. Andy loved it. There was a high level of humor and complexity that fit both artists.

Robert invited Andy and Qwerty to a party he was having the following week at his building on Lafayette Street. Qwerty was happy to be invited and indicated he would be there.

Andy always seemed to be looking around and observing people. He could be quiet for quite some time and then suddenly chatty over the smallest detail. Andy immediately suggested that they order the arugula salad.

"They use sliced Parmesan Reggiano and lightly seasoned olive oil and serve it with nicely toasted fresh French bread. The cheese is made in Italy by hand and aged at least twelve months. " Andy said with an air of satisfaction.

Qwerty loved the fact that Andy seemed to care about something as mundane as a salad and mused that some artists have eyes that see the unseen and know the unknowable. It required paying careful attention to what they saw in their everyday lives. Andy's keen sense of the importance of what most people took for granted was his mantra. He took soup cans from supermarket shelves to museum walls around the world. Qwerty felt honored to be exposed to Andy and his vision.

"Andy, why do they call your studio the Factory?"

Andy replied, "I grew up in Pittsburgh, which was a factory town. I didn't fit in and grew up as an outsider. Here in New York, I created my own factory. Now I fit in perfectly."

Andy said, "Please tell me more about yourself. I am sure it is an interesting story. "

Qwerty felt that he could share anything with Andy. He decided to tell him his early childhood story as he understood it and passed down to him over the years. Andy was a surprisingly good listener to the short version as they finished their lunch.

As Qwerty spoke, his mind drifted back to the longer version. The stories were indelibly written in his memory. His thoughts drifted back to thirty-five years ago, to the stories his adopted mother had repeated many times. She would spend hours telling him every detail of his arrival in her life. Each time that he heard the story, there would be another scene in the movie that played in the theater of his mind.

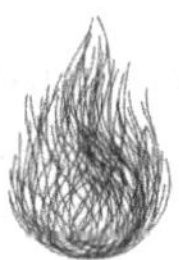

CHAPTER TWO

Headlights in the Darkness of an Upstate New York Snowstorm in 1946

Mary McClellan Hospital was located on a hilltop park overlooking a sleepy lower Adirondack village. The sprawling two-story brick building formed an institutional campus layout. Despite some pleasant landscaping, it had all the charm of an insane asylum. Nonetheless, the villagers and farmers from the surrounding countryside held Mary McClellan in high esteem. Rural hospitals are places of birth, death, and, in some cases, redemption. There were few patients or staff at the hospital this midwinter night during a snowstorm that some folks considered a blizzard. Most people in the area were hunkered down in their homes by a fire or curled up in bed, imitating the bears and going into hibernation. The local highway department was busy plowing the village streets if people were determined to brave the elements and drive. Lights in the distance were illuminating the falling snow in the village below.

In a small office lit only by a desk light and the ambient light of the outdoor lights of the portico that served as the hospital driveway entrance sat a middle-aged woman named Alice Smith. She wore horn-rimmed glasses, and her printed dress was suitable for a Norman Rockwell painting at Thanksgiving time. The office was drafty, and the darkness of the night seemed to enter through the window glass. She wrapped her fluffy sweater around her shoulders and was busy typing hospital forms assigned to her that afternoon. Alice worked at Mary McClellan in a variety of jobs under the title of head secretary. That title meant she did the paperwork and managed the front desk at off hours as she was that night. She also served as a Town Clerk for the surrounding township. Alice was a widow with no plans to remarry. Her marriage ended when her husband was killed in a barroom brawl at a pub called Snuffy's Tavern. He tended to be mean drunk. Alice managed to move on without him and found comfort in her faith and church group. The folks in her local Methodist church didn't think much of alcohol but didn't openly criticize those who drank too much. Alice would simply refer to alcoholics as people who shouldn't drink. Memories of her former husband did manage to return from time to time as they did that night. She sat at her desk that cold, dark night, typing and musing about her loneliness.

Snow in upstate New York can take many forms. Some snow falls straight down in tiny egg-shaped pellets that sting as they strike the skin. At other times, a storm brings big snowflakes that float gently in the night air and kiss the skin with drops of water. That night, the snowstorm created a universe of black with nothing but the white road and the large white flakes rocking back and forth from above. Looking out the window at the snow falling on the driveway distracted her from the typewriter keyboard. She was lost in counting the snowflakes and in the process her spirit was covered by them. The feeling was soothing.

The headlights from a pickup truck slowly entered the circular driveway leading to the hospital entrance. This type of old pickup was common in the town. What was once a shiny new truck from Detroit now had rusted fenders, a noisy muffler and dim headlights. The sparkling black paint was now a patina of colors and textures that only time and weather could create. The truck stopped for a moment at the entrance portico, moved a short distance, and then continued to the entry front steps. A young woman climbed out. She turned away from the wind and snow with a bundle in her arms, which she gently placed on the step, landing against the front door out of the wind. She then threw a scarf around her face and dashed back to the truck. She quickly slammed the passenger door. A few moments later, she opened the door again and put one foot on the ground, but an arm from inside the truck pulled her back in. Alice got up from her desk and stood looking out the window as the truck disappeared in the darkness. The red taillights faded in falling snow until they silently faded to black.

Alice threw her coat over her shoulders and opened the door as a gust of wind blew snow in the lobby. Turning her collar to the wind to reach down and pick up the bundle, she quickly closed the door behind her to keep out the storm. The bundle began to wiggle as she carried it back to her desk. She sat down, pulled the blanket back, and gazed upon a newborn baby boy. Despite the storm outside, he was serene. A young couple created the baby in a moment of passion, taking no responsibility for the future of their child. As Alice gazed at this twist of fate blown into her life by the winter storm, she felt warm inside. Her heart reached out to this snow-covered bundle and wrapped it in love. This baby was unplanned and unwanted by a teenage mother, then suddenly taken in by a surrogate mother who desperately needed to fill the void in her heart and life.

Her former husband's abuse had damaged Alice, but as time passed, all that faded into memory. She had been comforted in her relationship with a farmer named Adam Deedle. Adam had lost his wife years earlier. Alice and Adam had bonded at church services, and eventually, they moved in together at Alice's farm on the Battenkill. They were a bit ahead of their time in not wanting to marry. Her relationship with Adam gave her the confidence to take on new challenges in life. Holding this child against her breast awoke feelings that she had ignored to avoid admitting that something was missing in her relationship with Adam. Part of her wished the mother would return for her baby, yet another part wanted to hug this baby and never let go. He seemed in good health, and his diaper was clean. She took this time to have coffee and a cigarette and savor the moment. She gently placed the baby on the sofa near her desk and sang a verse of one of her favorite songs. "I don't want to set the world on fire; I just want to start a flame in your heart." This verse would be the mantra of this child's life.

Alice looked down at the bundle with its sleeping newborn and then out the window at the snow, which was now gently glowing in the driveway light as it fell from the darkness to the white blanket on the ground.

"Well, better do some paperwork on this boy and deal with the authorities in the morning when the storm breaks," Alice said to an imaginary person.

Alice sat down at the typewriter and inserted a birth certificate form. The date and time were easy. The mother was Jane Doe, and the father was John Doe. Everything seemed easy enough. The hard part was what to name this child. She started typing at the upper left-hand corner of the keyboard and stopped at "Y." "Q, W, E, R, T, Y, that works," she said to the same imaginary person. This baby now had an identity that only made sense to someone familiar with the typewriter keyboard. His last name was simply blank. Remembering her high school French class, she changed the k to C. Blanc works, she thought to herself. She typed Qwerty Blanc on the form in the space for the name.

Alice looked at the completed birth certificate, then down at the sleeping baby, and softly spoke, "Welcome to the world, Qwerty Blanc." Alice wasn't known for her sense of humor. Nonetheless, she looked around the room and laughed out loud. Even the imaginary person in the room must have found the name amusing.

The morning sun broke through the clouds as the storm departed. Qwerty slept peacefully through the night and awakened early. Alice located some formula in the nursery and gave him some breakfast.

She placed him in a nursery crib and greeted the usual hospital staff arriving for work.

One of the first to arrive was Doctor Carrol. He was a general practitioner who had spent his entire professional career serving the families of the village and surrounding community. He was a cheerful man who was sympathetic to the suffering of his patients. His strength and confidence healed people as much as his medicine. Alice took him up to the nursery, where Doctor Carrol pronounced the new arrival healthy as a honeybee on a dandelion.

Alice called the village police chief to let him know about the abandoned baby. She felt confident that once Chief Robertson was involved, the parents would be located, and the baby would be returned. Chief Robertson was called Robbie by everyone in the village. He was technically a police officer, but in this small community, his official duties were more aptly described as social work. The community endeared both Doctor Carrol and Chief Robbie. No one would question their judgment. They started the paperwork to document the discovery of the baby and to initiate the search for the parents. Doctor Carrol was content to look in on the baby and ensure that Alice was advised on keeping him in good health. He was confident that Alice and the nursing staff would take good care of the baby until the parents were located.

Chief Robbie's job normally entailed settling disputes among village neighbors over parking disputes, excessive teenage noise, public drinking, and occasionally the theft of a chainsaw. Seldom did the malfeasance in the village go beyond vandalism. In 1946 there were few resources and databases to investigate finding a baby abandoned by teenage parents. The young couple must have kept the birth a secret from their parents and their friends. In their minds, leaving the baby at Mary McClellan must have been an acceptable alternative to an abortion. Abortion was not an option in their world.

Chief Robbie's paperwork was sent to the State Police, and his deputies were sent out to ask questions about the parents throughout the area. There was no immediate response, and Chief Robbie could do nothing more but wait. The baby was safely in the care of the hospital, Alice, and Doctor Carrol. At this time, no one gave much thought about the ability of teenagers to be fit parents. That was a bridge to be crossed at the appropriate time. The focus was on simply locating them.

The next day, Alice returned to the hospital and was greeted by Chief Robbie.

"You realize, Alice, that we probably are not going to locate these kids who abandoned this baby. Poor little tyke will probably end up in an orphanage."

Alice was heartbroken at the thought that this little guy would be sent to an orphanage. "We can't let that happen," she said.

Chief Robbie replied, "Alice, we are just public servants. So often, we want to fix things, but sometimes, we must accept things the way they are."

Alice stamped her foot and said," Then this is just not one of those times!"

As the days passed Alice grew more attached to Qwerty to the point of obsession. A few days later, after finishing her morning shift as Town Clerk, she went to the hospital to check on Qwerty. Chief

Robbie and Doctor Carol were in the lobby discussing the status of the abandoned baby. Alice anxiously approached them.

"Any word on finding the parents?" Alice asked as she fidgeted with the side of her coat.

"Damned if we could find any clue as to the parents. Think it's time to hand him over to the social services." Chief Robbie said with a sad look on his face.

Alice looked at Doctor Carrol and pleaded, "Is there any chance I could take him home and care for him until the parents are located?"

"I can't think of a better place for him now. I don't think we would have a moment's peace until we told you that it would be okay."

"The Lord acts in mysterious ways. Adam and I are sure this baby was meant to be with us."

The next day, Alice and Adam arrived at the hospital after packing a box full of baby things in the trunk of their car. They prepared the spare bedroom with a crib and furniture to welcome their new addition. Alice cradled Qwerty in her arms as they drove home. She never wanted to let him go. This new family had just begun.

As the Town Clerk, she took matters into her own hands and filled out another birth certificate under the name Hank Smith. She loved Hank Williams' music and thought naming the baby after Hank would be sweet. She gave the baby a foster home until the legal process of adoption was complete. One day, the paperwork came through via registered mail. As far as Alice was concerned, Hank was officially hers and she would never let him go. Adam seemed ready and willing to be a father. Alice Smith and Adam Deedle shared parenting duties but decided to keep their relationship as it was.

They trusted each other and that was their bond. Adding Hank to their home would bond them closer. They sat at the dining table after dinner. Alice poured two cups of coffee into the usual mugs. Alice's mug noted home sweet home. Adam's mug asked about hugging a farmer today. In a cradle in the corner lay baby Hank with his toes in his mouth.

"Adam, you are a good man and I have feelings for you. If you help me raise this boy, you must promise me you will never hit the boy or me."

"Alice, I didn't get too far along in school, but I know a good deal when I see it."

So it was that Alice, Adam and Hank were now a family. Qwerty Blanc, aka Hank Smith, now had a home and two birth certificates. Consider calling it dual citizenship. His journey through life would have a fork in the road that required both.

<h1 style="text-align:center">Chapter Three</h1>

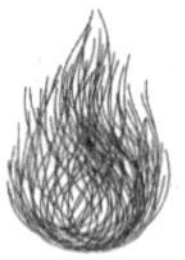

<h2 style="text-align:center">Time To Party</h2>

As evening set in on Prince Street, the streets of SoHo transitioned from the business of the day to the quiet of the night. The workers had returned home to the outer boroughs and the buildings were dark. Piles of cardboard obscured and blocked the sidewalk, waiting to be picked up by garbage trucks. The quiet streets were a stark contrast to the hustle and bustle of the commercial activity of the workday. If the day was a time to breathe in, then the night was a time to breathe out and prepare for the next breath.

Qwerty opened the door of his building on the corner of Prince and Greene Street and entered the deserted streets. He felt that the invitation to Rauschenberg's party was a sign of his acceptance of the social order of the art world. As he approached Lafayette

Street and the Rauschenberg building, he mused about Robert and the other artists he had observed over the past few years. Andy Warhol and the older generation of artists were the establishment. He understood that he was part of something new. Artists were categorized by labels that were convenient for critics and curators to fit their version of art history. Qwerty and his group were in a struggle to express themselves and their work. Their studios were sanctuaries. Exhibitions provided an opportunity to socialize and share ideas. Galleries, museums, collectors, and critics were a support system for art that also created the temptation to feed the ego, not the creative spirit of artists.

Qwerty never entirely understood why art writers and some curators grouped Robert in the same Pop Art category as Andy. Andy was the very essence of Pop, even in his personal life. However, Robert's work seemed much more complex. His work appeared to form a bridge from Abstract Expressionism to Pop. His painting, printmaking and assemblage were nuanced and even eccentric at times. His personality was charming, and his generosity to younger artists arriving on the scene was legend. Qwerty was delighted to be invited to this party. Robert was well-established at the Leo Castelli Gallery, exhibiting the best post-war modern artists. It became the gold standard for representing artists like Robert and Jasper Johns, but it also introduced the next generation of artists like Qwerty. That attention came from the international as well as the strictly American culture. SoHo was suddenly on the art world map.

Qwerty was excited as he rang the bell of the old rectory that was now Robert's New York headquarters. He joined a group of people waiting at the door. They were greeted by Hisachika Takahashi, Robert's long-time studio assistant and house manager. Hisachika was an artist in his own right and had become indispensable to Robert in creating new work. Qwerty had met him before, and he was convinced that Sashka, as Qwerty called him, was affected by the aji-no-moto he heaped on the food he prepared. Sashka considered aji-no-moto health food and swore by it. Americans called it MSG and used it sparingly due to the side effects. Sashka's unusual manic behavior contrasted with Rauschenberg's laid-back Texas charm. They were also greeted by a box turtle that roamed free in the building. It was ancient and had managed to avoid getting stepped on over the years. Everything about Robert and his lifestyle was bigger than life to Qwerty. The turtle was just one of many giveaways that this artist was indeed not cut from the typical American cloth despite his Texas upbringing.

The guests made their way upstairs to a modest loft setting that was not the art studio Qwerty was expecting. The building was originally an old five-story brick church rectory that included a chapel annex in the back of the lot. Artists were repurposing SoHo buildings in ways the original occupants never imagined. Some artists used the high ceilings and open spaces to add theater and grandeur to their work and their identity. The former rectory and chapel lost its solemn religious mantra to become a playground of Robert's imagination. He had converted the building into a residence for himself and a variety of support spaces for his work and a small staff. Robert also owned a work studio in Captiva, an island off the Gulf Coast of Florida. He divided his time between this island studio and his headquarters at the rectory in New York City. These locations, as well as locations around the world, were studios for Robert's boundless energy and inspiration. The chapel was a work in progress. It was a chrysalis awaiting transformation into a butterfly. Qwerty imagined that this grand space would someday be converted to space for significant works waiting for Robert's imagination to create.

Artist's lofts were made for parties, and Robert's was no exception. The music was loud, and people were dancing. The space served as a gallery for a collection of artwork by his friends. Any museum would be happy to exhibit the works in the gallery if they were available from Robert's collection. A large Franz Kline abstract expressionist painting caught Qwerty's eye. He stood in front of the large black brush strokes slashing across the white background of the painting with evident admiration. He loved the feeling generated by abstract expressionism. For him, Kline's sparse but powerful brush strokes hit the nail on the proverbial head. Robert came over, holding a drink, and put his arm around him. His arm was warm and reassuring.

Robert smiled and asked, "Do you like that painting?"

"It is powerful and angry," Qwerty replied.

Robert looked at him, smiled, and said, "I'll never forget being at an opening with Franz Kline when that painting was first shown. A group of people were standing around gazing at it and said something to the effect that any child could have painted that. Franz walked over to them and said, Yes, but that child wouldn't know when to stop."

They laughed as Robert turned to his other guests. He moved among the guests like a bee pollinating a field of clover. Qwerty moved to the bar to get something to make him a bit more sociable. The bar was stocked with top-shelf whiskey brands. Qwerty ordered a Makers Mark on the rocks. Over the years, he acquired a taste for good bourbon. The crowd grew until the room was filled with people admiring each other, chatting and dancing.

Qwerty was standing at the bar admiring one of Robert's paintings when he heard someone laughing. As he turned to see who was amused, he was immersed in the most beautiful big brown eyes he had ever seen. The eyes were just the beginning of the beauty of Yolanda Jones. Yolanda was a law student attending New York University. Her parents had immigrated to New York from the Philippines in the early 1950s. They were both successful middle-class professionals who provided the best for their daughter. She was an ethnic mix of Spanish and Chinese that marriages in the Philippines often created. Yolanda was sophisticated and cultured with the presence and awareness of an urban cat. Her eyes commanded attention. Her straight, jet-black hair starkly contrasted with her smooth, clear skin. Everything about her was sensual, even how she moved through time and space.

Yolanda was standing in front of a large abstract painting with thick brush strokes of varying color. Two old table fans with wire cages were mounted on the upper corners, oscillating back and forth. Robert loved to rummage through antique markets to find objects like the fans to use in his work.

She said, "That is so funny. The fans are drying the paint."

Turning to Qwerty, she said, "Hi, I am Yolanda. How do you know Robert?"

After fortifying himself again with another sip, he replied," Qwerty Blanc. I only know Robert through the gallery that shows our work. I love how Robert takes old junk into his work and gives it new life. He can take old newspapers or cardboard, add a few brushstrokes of paint, and turn it into an urban streetscape. I am not that clever. I just like to see junk burn."

Yolanda brightened and said, "I know who you are. You're the artist who set that Greene Street building on fire a few years back. You disappeared for some time."

"That building fire wasn't my fault. I left the scene back then because I was drafted into the Army shortly after that fire. I suppose you could say that I paid my debt to society. Anyway, I am back in action. If you give me your number, I'll tell you the whole story."

Qwerty wrote her telephone number on his arm as she joined a boyish-looking girl standing near the entry and drifted off into the crowd.

Qwerty loved to dance as people on the dance floor grooved with him. He remembered a family friend who spent summers in his hometown and lived in the city invited him to see a performance of Stars and Stripes by the New York City Ballet for the inauguration of Governor Nelson Rockefeller. The performance was in Albany and promised to be an adventure for young Hank at the time. He marveled that a male dancer could appear to leave Mother Earth and fly. When Hank returned from the performance, he bounded about Adam's field, leaping and spinning in the air. Ballet had struck a chord in his imagination. His upstate village had no outlet for his desire to dance. The nail in the coffin for his ballet fantasies came immediately. He asked Adam if he could learn ballet. Adam replied that ballet was for sissies, with no further comment.

He saw the darkness of small-town limitations and was open to the light of something new. He loved Jack London's book "Call of the Wild" and felt his own call of the wild whenever he had a chance to wade down a stream and lose himself in the woods. His studio in SoHo had replaced the woods as a place of refuge and renewal. As Qwerty danced, he felt everything in motion and as it was meant to be.

The party continued until midnight. Robert and some of his friends had quietly disappeared. Qwerty and most of the remaining group walked down Lafayette Street to Chambers Street. They made their way to the West Side Highway and eventually to Mickey's Bar.

Mickey's Bar was located in one of the few buildings on the West Side of Lower Manhattan that remained spared from demolition. Urban development was in progress, and most previously existing buildings had been demolished just north of the World Trade Center site. The bar was dark and noisy and smelled like old orange peels. The floor was covered with wood shavings. It was perfect for after-hours drinking and drugging. The term "getting on a mission" was used to mean getting wasted on drugs and alcohol. Qwerty decided to get on a mission and lost himself in the crowd. He extended his night by snorting a few lines of cocaine that were conveniently left on the top of the toilet tank. He thanked the neighborhood boys in the bathroom for sharing the drugs.

The long walk back to Prince Street was filled with thoughts of seeing Yolanda again and how dark that part of the city was despite the streetlights. There was a strange pleasure in being a bit drunk and consumed by the anonymity of the urban darkness guided only by an occasional landmark and streetlight.

Chapter Four

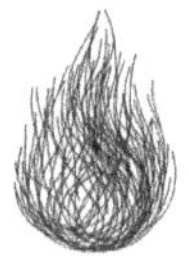

Yolanda

Qwerty's post-party hangover lasted a few days, but the telephone number on his arm still burned like a brand. He finally got the courage to call and arrange a dinner date. The first thought that came to mind was having dinner in Chinatown. It didn't occur to him that just because Yolanda looked exquisitely oriental meant she liked Chinese food. His social learning curve was indeed steep. Male adolescence in rural America can only be described as a gauntlet of guilt, glands, and aggression to conceal the fear. To make matters worse, he seemed to have no one to talk to about his sexual or romantic feelings. This was true in his hometown and even worse in New York City, where he was embarrassed even to admit he knew nothing about relationships with women. By regularly going to openings and Saturday afternoon bar gatherings, he was beginning to have more meaningful conversations with women on the edge of social change. His relationship with other men was also a work in progress. His art world contemporaries seemed more interested in how to pay the rent or to get a gallery to show their work. They gave their opinion on social issues only if they had time to talk about anything but themselves.

Qwerty rehearsed his phone call to Yolanda as he paced around his studio. When he finally got the courage to dial her number, he forgot everything he had rehearsed.

"Hi Yolanda, it's Qwerty. Would you like to get some Chinese food tomorrow evening?" he said nervously.

"Of course, I would like to meet with you tomorrow evening, but I was hoping we could go out dancing. You are a terrific dancer. Perhaps another time?"

"Great idea. I wish I had thought of that. We could meet at seven o'clock in front of Dave's Corner at Canal and Broadway if that works for you." Qwerty said with crossed fingers.

"Just don't set the restaurant on fire. Sorry, I couldn't resist that one."

"I promise to be on my best behavior. See you then," Qwerty said with a sigh of relief.

He spent the next hour feeling slightly humiliated. Women are just too mysterious, he thought. Meet an attractive woman. Put foot in mouth. Repeat. This was his mantra, he thought to himself. Chinatown was really a bad idea, he thought, but that is where they were going. Dating would remain challenging. At least he learned that women might enjoy dancing, watching shows, and even reading poetry.

They walked by the park off Bayard Street just south of Canal Street. Old men were playing board games, and a young woman was burning things from paper bags and offering prayers for good fortune. People were exercising and practicing Tai Chi to music only they could hear. Walking down the winding streets, they passed dozens of storefronts selling fresh produce, odds and ends from the Orient, and even an oddly placed small Catholic Church. Qwerty loved being in Chinatown almost as much as in the West Village and Central Park. All these enclaves in New York City were populated with new people in his life from faraway places. They brought with them a taste of their homeland's sights, smells and sounds.

The restaurant Excellent Dumpling had excellent scallion pancakes, but the dumplings were not excellent by any stretch of the imagination. Qwerty picked a small booth in the corner that was not directly under the fluorescent lights. Yolanda looked great in any light, but Qwerty was a bit insecure about how he looked in this light. They sat down to order.

The server was typical for Chinatown. He was succinct to the point that he was either going to rush to the kitchen to get the food order or pull out a knife and plunge it into the customer. This was a far cry from the waitresses at the Chit Chat Cafe in Qwerty's hometown. They served the food but were more interested in discovering all the gossip they could gather and share with their customers.

Qwerty and Yolanda settled on some appetizers and dinner and placed their order. The waiter jotted something down and mumbled in Mandarin as he walked to the kitchen window opening.

Yolanda said "I love visiting and love the food, but I have never been comfortable with naming this area Chinatown. It is the equivalent of having a section of Hong Kong called Whitey Town. Perhaps I am sensitive to these tags because I identify as an Asian American."

When the waiter returned, Qwerty said, "Hey, how about those Mets?" He chuckled as if he just scored one for the home team. "What is it with Chinese waiters, Yolanda? They have a nasty attitude."

Yolanda replied. "Maybe they are the metaphor for being an Asian in this country. You wouldn't have a clue. White males like you take their status for granted and are clueless about how offensive little comments and actions can be. I am an Asian woman. I see it from the valley of the mountain that you guys are perched upon. I am going to be a lawyer, but I will still have to push this burden up the slope."

"You are right, Yolanda. As a woman, you have to work even harder. There are exceptional women artists that I have talked to who have mentioned how hard it is for a woman to get recognition. What I am hearing is that you feel being an Asian woman is even tougher. OK, I get it."

Yolanda reached her hand across the table to his and smiled. "How about those Mets?"

The small town where he grew up had no diversity, so he wasn't aware there was a problem. The city seemed so diverse that he found other races and cultures interesting and not threatening. Neither environment generated mean-spirited and harmful prejudice in him. He remembered his days in the Army, where the Vietnamese were referred to as Gooks. It never crossed his mind where terms like that came from and the hatred it produced. He preferred to call them Charlie as if that was a nicer term in his mind.

After eating some of the best sesame noodles and scallion pancakes in town, they agreed to try something they both had never had. They ordered the Special Peking Duck for two, which was a big mistake. The duck entrée tasted as bad as the ducks hanging in the window of the restaurant looked. The dinner was educational at best, but their conversation was lively, and they both enjoyed each other's company. Qwerty realized how lucky he was to be having dinner with such a beautiful and intelligent woman. He also knew that she was way beyond his reach and that he should savor the brief time he might spend with her.

Walking back to Yolanda's apartment on King Street, they stopped off at Fanelli's Bar on Prince Street for drinks. As usual, Fanelli's was cool, dark, loud and packed with patrons. Fanelli's Bar was one of the oldest continuously operated bars in the city. Very little had been altered over the years, and the patina of the paint on the walls and woodwork was comforting. When it was busy, it had the ambient sound of a Wall Street trading floor. Fanelli's was a place to drink and join the soundtrack. Yolanda was able to drink and chat with the best of the boys. They were both quickly at the center of a group of regulars at the bar.

After realizing that they would rather be alone, they drifted off to a corner in the side room to talk more intimately. There was talk about Yolanda's future as a lawyer and there was talk of Qwerty's upcoming art exhibits. Then, there was not much talk at all. They found each other touching without even being aware of it. Yolanda whispered in his ear something about walking her home. They kissed and walked out the door to the sidewalk.

Yolanda's apartment was vintage Greenwich Village with exposed brick walls, hanging pots in an open kitchen, wood floors with throw rugs and the usual collection of succulent plants and ferns. Makeshift bookshelves created by wooden milk crates were stacked against the brick wall. The titles of the books reflected an eclectic taste in subject matter. Some books were obviously from the law school, while others were by local Village writers like Jack Kerouac and Alan Ginsberg. The studio apartment appeared comfortably spacious. The furniture consisted of a table with chairs and a mattress on the floor. Yolanda went to the kitchen and opened a bottle of wine. Qwerty sat at the table and rolled a joint.

"I prefer to be with women, but I am attracted to you, so let's just go with it." Yolanda said, passing him a glass of red wine.

Qwerty stripped and stretched out on the mattress. She sat beside him and gently ran her hands over his face and then his body. Her eyes were the center of Qwerty's universe. She stood up and took off her clothes, looking down at Qwerty. Her skin was flawless and tan. Her hair cascaded down her shoulders onto her back. When her breasts were free of her bra, they swayed down on her chest gently from side to side. Qwerty was frozen physically and in time. Yolanda slowly mounted him and when he felt himself inside her he wanted time to stand still. He knew that when she withdrew, he might never experience her again.

"Close your eyes and put your hands on my chest. Can you feel my heart pounding?" Qwerty whispered.

"It is a drum beat for us." Yolanda whispered back.

For that moment in time, she was his woman, and it was not a fantasy. When he could hold back no longer, he felt himself pouring into her. They didn't move for a long while. She had allowed him to experience her as a woman. He just wanted to stay with her as long as he could.

They curled up on the mattress with a blanket and lit the joint. The talk was easy now. Qwerty gently caressed and massaged Yolanda. She seemed to share the closeness that he felt.

As Qwerty began to tell Yolanda about his career she became increasingly interested in his early time in the Village. She asked him to start at the very beginning and not skip any parts. Qwerty realized that even though he was overwhelmed by the events of his career that telling the story was fun. They drank and talked into the night cradled on that mattress.

Qwerty's mind drifted back to 1964 when he graduated high school and caught a New York Central Train from Saratoga Springs to Penn Station and the adventure of New York City. Yolanda faded from his consciousness as he stared at the ceiling and began describing his journey to Greenwich Village and the chain of events that led to and propelled his career in art.

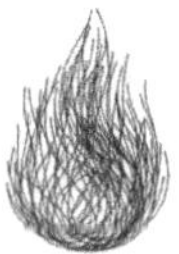

CHAPTER FIVE

Greenwich Village 1964

Qwerty thoughts carried him back in time to his first encounter with the world of New York City. There are places on the planet that can welcome like no other. They provide the same feeling as our reaction to an adoring grandmother offering a homemade cookie fresh from her oven. Greenwich Village welcomed Qwerty.

The train from Saratoga Springs to New York Penn Station gave him a sense of transition. The view of the Hudson River out the window was scenic and soothing. When he arrived at Penn Station, he was shocked to see a construction site. The glorious structure, with its majestic steel arches and carved stone pillars, was almost completely gone.

The transition from the remaining part of the train station to the subway system was quite straightforward. Qwerty studied the subway map. "Seems easy enough. East, West, North, and South. Street numbers go up towards the North. Eastside is east of 5th Avenue, and Westside is west of 5th Avenue. The avenues run north and south. Got it. The Bronx is up and the Battery's down for whatever that's worth."

The "A" train was a subway train at Penn Station. It had a direct line to the heart of Greenwich Village. He found the site of Washington Square Park and took the downtown express to West 4th Street, which exited near the park.

From the moment he exited the West 4th Street subway stop, he was treated to the sights, sounds and smells of Greenwich Village. He was puzzled that the subway stop was labeled West 4th Street but exited onto West 8th Street. He would soon learn that nothing about the geography of the streets in Greenwich Village was logical. West 10th Street crossed West 4th Street. The streets were meant to confuse people who didn't belong there in the first place. As he walked east on 8th Street, he saw the great stone arch at the beginning of 5th Avenue, marking the entry of Washington Square Park. As he passed under and through the arch, he entered the park to the fountain. The great circular stone fountain seemed powerful to him with its water and glorious gathering of people. A lively crowd was sitting on its circular bench and standing around the perimeter. He was reminded of when a traveling circus came to his small town. The transient characters of the circus fascinated him. Where did they come from, what did they talk about, and where are they going? At last, he had discovered the place where magical characters dwell. Guitar players, poets and nearly extinct beatniks were there in great numbers. On the edge of the crowd were jugglers and the clowns as a finishing touch to the array.

A shabby but noble-looking black man beckoned to him, "Hey, Jim."

He was unaware that the term "Jim" was code for "white guy." This was all new to him, so he replied, "My name is Hank …I mean Qwerty -not Jim."

"Okay, Jim. That's cool. Can you help me out?" he said, holding out a paper cup.

Qwerty didn't have any money but decided to ask his new acquaintance about a place to live. "Do you know where I can find an apartment in the neighborhood?"

He stood smiling, waiting for a response to his question. The old man lunged at him and snarled, "Do I look like a fucking real estate agent to you?"

Qwerty jumped back and realized that getting the hang of city life was going to take some time. He continued through the park to the Sullivan Street corner section, where men were playing chess. They seemed quite serious. There was a tournament atmosphere, but the rules and hierarchy were only known to the ancient spirits of the park.

As he exited onto Sullivan Street, a group of men played dominoes around a folding table on the sidewalk. They were as lively and noisy as the chess players were sullen and quiet. When he approached Bleecker Street, another group of middle-aged men were hanging out on the sidewalk outside a storefront with a red, white, and green sign that read The Sullivan Street Social Club. When he looked up, he could see the remnants of little lights and pennants from last year's street celebration.

Through the dirty windows, he could see that the social club's interior was dark and uninviting. The group outside seemed to be engaging everyone on the street sidewalk, in stark contrast to the quiet club inside. Qwerty introduced himself to a man with incredibly thick eyeglasses and greased-down black hair. The others called him Sali. Sally was a girl's name, he thought, but shrugged it off as just another city thing.

He asked, "Sorry to bother you, but do you know where I could find a vacant apartment in the neighborhood?"

Sali replied, "Do I look like a fucking real estate agent to you?" Qwerty was getting the hang of this, so he thanked him and started to walk away. "Hey kid, an NYU student just moved out of a studio in that corner building. Ring the super."

Qwerty was encouraged. "Thanks, Sali."

He walked to the corner building. It was a modest four-story brick apartment building. The proximity to Bleecker Street meant there would be much more street noise. Bleecker Street was home to a bar frequented by a motorcycle gang known as the Hell's Angels, who quartered in the East Village but socialized on Bleecker Street. As a result, the tenants were mostly NYU students who rented apartments for their time at the school. After ringing the bell, he was greeted by the building superintendent holding a small wire sculpture and dangling a lit cigarette from his mouth. His first-floor apartment doubled as an apartment and wire sculpture studio. He wore round spectacles and his hair seemed to emanate from the center of his face as if driven by static electricity.

"Don't tell me; you are looking for a pad."

Qwerty replied, "Yes, I am. Sali said you might have something. Do you have anything?"

"Sali sent you? Okay, apartment 2F is available. I need $50.00 security and $50.00 rent due on the first of the month. Here is the key."

Qwerty settled with the super and opened the door of 2F. He was happy to see a pleasant studio with a kitchenette and bathroom and a window with a fire escape landing on Sullivan Street.

"Welcome to Greenwich Village and freedom," he said to himself, both hands in the air. "Goodbye, Hank Smith, average guy, and hello, Qwerty Blanc artiste."

His only possessions were a small suitcase filled with clothes and a case with his fiddle. After hanging his clothes and unpacking his suitcase, he grabbed his fiddle case and headed out the door. Most of his teenage high school classmates in his hometown listened to AM radio, which played an eclectic mix of rock and roll. Fortunately, Alice and Adam had taken him to live music performances at local venues and to square dances. His taste in music was a blend of these sources. Adam Deedle had given him an exceptional fiddle that had been passed down to him from his father. One day, he drove young Hank to the nearby town of White Creek to meet Stonewall Robertson. Stonewall got his name from his trade as a stone mason, but he was a legend as a fiddle player. Stonewall had big, sad blue eyes on a face lined in the wrinkles created by smiles and the great outdoors. The lessons were a monthly treat that lasted years. Hank would sneak into the back of Snuffy's Tavern on the state highway on Saturday nights to hear the fiddle contests and dance music. Stonewall would invite him to join in from time to time when young Hank was old enough to fit in.

Fiddle case in hand, Hank Smith, now Qwerty Blanc, walked west on Bleecker Street, ready for adventure. Stonewall had mentioned that Alan Block was an excellent fiddler and teacher. He told him to look up Alan when he got to Greenwich Village. Alan had a shoe business and hosted music sessions in the back of his store.

It was Saturday, and Bleecker Street was filling up with parked motorcycles from the Hell's Angels. He enjoyed walking past espresso bars, falafel stands, and craft shops, which were homespun and surprisingly comforting to him. He stopped to listen to a young street musician with curly hair playing guitar and harmonica at the park opposite the Pioneer Market on 6th Avenue and Bleecker. He thought, "This guy is good, maybe even as good as Woody Guthrie."

During a break, he asked, "Do you know where I can find Alan Block?"

He replied, "Everybody knows Alan. He can be found behind his boot and sandal store on the Avenue."

Qwerty said, "Thanks. Hey man, you are good. I love your songs. Very original and smart. What is your name?"

He replied, "They often call me Speedo, but my real name is Mr. Earl." Qwerty recognized this lyric from a Doo Whop song on the AM radio.

"Okay, I get it, wise guy," Qwerty muttered to himself as he made his way to Alan Block's shop.

When he arrived at Alan's shop, a man in coveralls and a railroad hat was leaving with a new pair of sandals in hand. A man with a welcoming sense of hospitality was turning the door sign from open to closed.

He looked at Qwerty's fiddle case and said, "You must be here for the workshop; come on in."

"My teacher, Stonewall Robertson, told me about you and said I should look you up when I got to the Village."

"Stonewall!? Geez, I haven't seen him in years. I would visit him during the summers I spent up there. I would show him some tunes and he would show me how to get those tunes rocking. Introduce yourself and join right in."

They went to a back room where a group of people were tuning their fiddles, mandolins, banjos and guitars. Other than their choice of instruments, they appeared to have very little in common. Half were middle-aged or beyond, and the other half were teenagers. The musicians shared a passion for old-timey music. The old-timey music, as it was called, wasn't played on the average radio, and it was not on the radar even for kids interested in popular folk music. It was initially based in Appalachia and had its own distinctive rhythms and structure. Some of the tunes were gospel, but most were made for dance. People like Alan Block collected the tunes from Library of Congress recordings and obscure Appalachian musicians still performing. They were keeping it alive and passed on to young musicians. Qwerty sat down and rosined up his bow.

Alan grabbed his fiddle and announced, "Let's warm up with Soldiers Joy."

Soldiers Joy was the universal tune for fiddlers to play at informal gatherings. Legend has it that soldier's joy was slang for drugs that numbed the pain of war. It is a tune that everyone seemed to know and love. It was the first tune that Stonewall had taught Qwerty as a child. Immediately, Qwerty felt at ease in the group. The older musicians took turns calling out a tune and demonstrating licks they had picked up over the years. A few brought sheet music, but most of the tunes were learned by ear. Qwerty was surprised at how fast the teenagers could grasp the essence of these old-time melodies. Qwerty felt right at home.

When the session was over, there was time to socialize and drink apple cider. A few stepped outside to roll what Qwerty thought were Bugle cigarettes. To avoid calling attention to pot smoking, smokers would buy Bugle tobacco that came with its own rolling paper. They could easily use the same paper to roll what they called a joint. They substituted marijuana for Bugler tobacco and avoided being caught.

Smoking pot was new to Qwerty, but he immediately enjoyed the buzz. He found himself laughing and engaged in lively conversation with his new-found friends. He mentioned that he needed to find some work, and a young musician named Steve said that he had just gotten a full-time job at the new guitar store on Bleecker Street. Steve said that he was repairing instruments and that the store was a great place to learn and work. Steve also said he had been helping with installations and general gallery work at the Green Gallery. Steve suggested that Qwerty talk to them about filling his old job at the gallery. He gave Qwerty a note with the information and told him to say that Steve recommended him. Qwerty knew very little about art galleries, but the work that Steve described sounded perfect for his skill set. Adam Deedle had spent countless hours teaching him to do carpentry, plumbing and electrical work. Farmers never had the money to hire out this type of work, so they learned the skills out of necessity. Qwerty realized that working at an art gallery doing the type of work that matched his general skill set might be a good fit. He thanked Steve for the lead and promised to stay in touch.

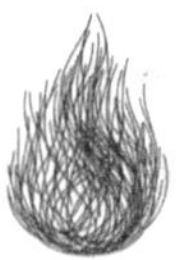

CHAPTER SIX

Track Lighting and Gallery Walls

The following morning, Qwerty arrived at the Green Gallery. The gallery was initially located downtown as an artist-run cooperative gallery on East 10th Street in the East Village. The Green Gallery was now owned by its director and relocated to midtown Manhattan on 57th Street. The neighboring midtown galleries were larger and exhibited artworks that were generally international and more established in the art marketplace. The Green Gallery was one of the new arrivals in midtown that exhibited avant-garde art. The visitors to the downtown gallery wore coveralls and sandals. The new location attracted a more sophisticated clientele. These patrons included elegant, tall blond women wearing designer shoes with sensible medium-height heels.

The elevator from the street-level lobby opened into a large white space with simple white light fixtures mounted on tracks flush with the ceiling. There was a reception area at the entry. The doors to other rooms were hidden from view in openings in the walls. The design was intended to emphasize the art exhibit immediately. Qwerty entered the gallery and approached the reception counter. An attractive young woman sat behind the counter, arranging photo slides and paperwork.

"My name is Qwerty Blanc. Steve said that he used to work here and that you might need someone to take his old job. He said that I should talk to Richard."

"I am sorry Richard is very busy. Just leave your telephone number, and we will get back to you." She added, "Sorry that it is so dark in here, but the lighting isn't working."

Qwerty saw an opportunity to show that he had something to offer. In high school, Qwerty worked summers helping a neighboring electrician and became proficient at electrical repairs.

He said, "Where is your electrical breaker panel? Maybe I can help."

The receptionist took Qwerty to the utility room at the back of the gallery. He found the breaker that was tripped and quickly realized what was wrong. He saw far too many lights on some of the lighting tracks. He removed a few extra lights from the track on the problem circuit. The gallery lighting was restored.

Richard came out of his office. He was not much older than Qwerty, with spectacles, curly hair, and the fashion style of an Ivy

League college professor. He approached the receptionist and said, "Thank God you found an electrician. We have an opening tonight."

The receptionist replied, "I couldn't reach the electrician, but this nice young man had fixed the problem. He said he was hoping to take over Steve's old job."

Richard replied, "You are hired and can start now."

In the following months, Qwerty enjoyed the variety of work at the gallery. The steady employment and daily commute allowed him to explore the city and the art scene. He met the best and brightest young artists who frequented the gallery. He quickly realized that the artists represented at the gallery were outliers. There was no shortage of art schools in the city, like the Art Students League and a variety of college art schools, but most of the artists he met had no formal art education. Each day, he felt more comfortable meeting new people and exploring new places. His identity as Hank Smith was fading into the past.

Qwerty spent time after work at either Fanelli's Bar or Cedar Tavern, frequented by some gallery artists. He spent time with a group of people who considered themselves part of a movement in art later to be named Fluxus, based on the consensus of curators and art historians. All the artists in Fanelli's and the Cedar Bar had one thing in common: They liked to drink.

One night at Fanelli's, a large hand shook his shoulder. The hand belonged to Claus. He had a mild manner, but he was a physically imposing figure. He stood about six foot three with shoes that seemed to be at least size fifteen. Richard considered him one of his favorite artists and his career seemed to be taking off. Claus was someone who took a personal interest in Qwerty. Qwerty's service position wasn't important enough for most artists and patrons to pay much attention. There were others who sensed that anyone working in an art gallery might lead to a creative career. A gallery service job was considered to be an apprenticeship by the workers. Claus had a generous spirit and seemed to appreciate Qwerty's skills and competence in his gallery work. He sensed there was more to Qwerty than his job.

"Qwerty. We are having a quick happening show at a vacant building on Greene Street. Come join us."

"Thanks for asking, but at the moment, I don't have any artwork to exhibit."

Claus replied, "You wouldn't be the first person to jump in without any work ready to show.

That is the fun of what we do in these pop-up shows. They are just happenings."

"You're on!" Qwerty said with a smile.

Claus picked up the bar tab and suggested they go check out the location of the pop-up show. The streets were deserted as they often were in the evening. When he and Claus got to the Greene Street building, an artist was holding a chicken under a grated area in the sidewalk near the building entry.

"That's Vito," Claus said, "Don't know the chicken's name."

They laughed as Vito continued to get his happening piece rehearsed.

"Home sweet home," Qwerty thought to himself as he looked down at the chicken. Qwerty remembered sitting in Adam's old barn reading a passage from Shakespeare that he was required to read for an English class to a chicken. The chicken didn't have a clue about Shakespeare but seemed to be paying rapt attention.

They entered the cavernous storefront space, which formerly held textile shelves and workers who sat at long tables and machines. The sixteen-foot ceilings exaggerated the space's emptiness, with its abandoned remnants and peeling calcified coating on the plaster walls. There was a flurry of activity as people set up art around the room and up and down the walls.

"How do I know if I can use a spot?" Qwerty asked.

Claus said, "There are no rules here. As I said, it is a happening. They aren't organized by any group or person. They just seem to happen."

Claus left Qwerty to visit with other artists.

"What the heck. I guess I should let something happen." Qwerty said to himself.

On a shelf, there was a box of old candles and some string. He lit candles and placed them geometrically in a vacant corner. Attaching some string from different points on the wall, he created a triangular special boundary. The string defined space for his work, and the flame of the candles provided the center of energy. He wrote Qwerty Blanc on the wall and realized that he had just become Qwerty Blanc, the artist. He enjoyed his first experience being a part of this happening.

Richard and his silent partner from the gallery attended the pop-up show. They stood in a corner and seemed to be having a lively conversation about Qwerty's improvised artwork. They were joined by an artist named Dan, who had created small sculptures with incandescent lights. He heard them saying something about the essence of vision created by light. Claus claimed there were no rules, but these loosely grouped young artists seemed to know what was acceptable. Repeating the past was unacceptable. The string and flame were new and acceptable. Qwerty had no idea how this moment and his exchanges with these artists would change his life. It was indeed a "Happening."

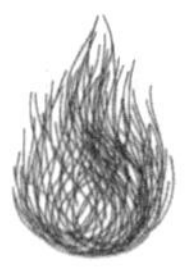

CHAPTER SEVEN

Come on Baby Light My Fire

A few months after the pop-up show, Qwerty entered the Green Gallery as usual but was called into Richard's conference office. Richard and his silent partner were sitting on the sofa. Normally, any meetings in a conference room were private, and it was unusual for Richard to invite Qwerty into the room. He asked him to sit down in a chair nearby. Qwerty was nervous that he might have done something wrong.

"We are planning our annual end-of-the-season invitational show before the summer break. Qwerty, we were wondering if you would like to create some pieces for the show here at the gallery. We thought your piece at the pop-up show was spot on. Claus said we need to encourage new talent. He was referring to you, of course."

Qwerty burst into a big smile and replied, "That is fantastic, Richard. Right on!"

"Just give us some idea of what you are going to do. We can fit you in the small back room."

After work, Qwerty headed straight for the Cedar Tavern to drink and talk this out with the people he considered real artists. He felt as though he had just received his club membership.

Hank Smith grew up with no plan, ambition, or desire to be an important figure in the world. As Qwerty Blanc in the 1960s New York City, he developed plans and ambition, and was comfortable becoming an important figure in the art world. Qwerty felt that he didn't know much, but knew what mediocrity felt like. As a teenager, Hank detested being average, although being average was a comfort zone. His identity as an artist allowed him to go beyond average and redefine his comfort zone. There was a welcoming sense of belonging to something new. He didn't know how he would fit in, but he wanted to belong.

His chats with artists at the bars produced no new ideas and the show was just a month away. His candles and pop-up work created some interest, but there had to be more. He needed inspiration for something that would be worthy of being in Richard's gallery. He was hoping a muse would give him a signal. Since Greek gods didn't appear to be available, he set out to find some spirits in New York City. With that in mind, he walked through SoHo and then onto Canal Street. He decided to stop at the sidewalk stand at Dave's Corner for a snack. There was a large grey-haired man wearing a filthy apron and smoking a short cigar, serving quick treats at the counter.

" I'll have a knish with mustard and vanilla egg cream," Qwerty said, wondering if his knish would have ashes as well as mustard.

"Well, that's original," the guy said, wiping his hands on his apron.

"Thanks, Groucho," Qwerty replied, allowing himself a moment to realize that he was getting the hang of being a New Yorker.

Once Qwerty had his treats, he headed East on Canal Street toward Chinatown in search of dinner. When he reached Mulberry Street, there were ducks hanging in the window of a restaurant. The naked ducks hung by their necks were slowly turning color from the pale of death to a pleasant amber. The famous Peking Duck dish at restaurants requires this process to remove the excess water and remaining fat and tighten the skin. Qwerty looked at the ducks and then into the kitchen area beyond.

In contrast to this slow processing of the ducks, the cooks were a flurry of activity. They vigorously tossed up dinners in their large, very hot woks. He was fascinated at how they launched the vegetables and meats airborne as the hot flames reached upward to catch the mist in the air. The cook closest to him heated his empty wok and sprinkled the heated metal with droplets of water. The wok sizzled and came to life with a tremendous burst of steam and flames.

"That's it!" Qwerty hollered. "Fire and rain!"

People on the sidewalk moved away while cautiously eyeing him. In New York City, strange behavior and occasional utterances usually are ignored. A loud outburst from someone on the street gets people's attention, even if that attention is brief.

He was so excited that he got his dinner to go and hurried back to his apartment on Sullivan Street. He had trouble getting to sleep. He rolled a joint, ate some raisin bread for dessert, and relaxed. He lay back, imagining a wok in the center of a small gallery room with a camp burner under it with water dripping from the ceiling. The water would burst into steam. The wok and the device for heating it required modification to become a sculpture. His observation of art at the gallery had given him access to the tools he needed to transform everyday objects into gallery objects. The handles from the wok would have to go and he would need a cylinder to conceal the heating device. The water coming from the ceiling would require the source and tubing to be concealed. As a final touch, he imagined stones being placed on the floor in a circle around the wok. He drifted off to sleep quite pleased with himself.

The following day, he awoke to the sound of the apartment doorbell.

"Nobody ever comes here. Must be some nonsense." He said to himself.

To his surprise, an artist he befriended from the gallery stood at his door with a camera in hand. His name was Nomo. He was born in Japan but grew up in New York City after his parents were able to immigrate to America after World War II. He was fascinated by television and was exploring the medium for ideas for his own art filming and performing. Nomo was convinced that video cameras would be available at some point for artists outside the world of television to use. For the moment, he went everywhere with his

Kodak Super 8 camera, documenting the world he inhabited in New York City.

"Q-man, let's head down to Chinatown for some fun. I want to make a film about freeing a blue crab being sold in the live street market from the horrors of being boiled alive."

"Wow! That's perfect. I can show you my idea for the piece I am putting in the summer invitational show at the Green Gallery. They offered me the back room. I was in a panic, but I think I have finally got something perfect."

"Far-out Q-man, let's go!"

When they reached the restaurant with the dripping ducks on Canal Street, Nomo looked at the ducks hanging by their necks and said, "I suppose the poor ducks are being made an example so that other ducks won't commit the same crime."

Qwerty laughed and then pointed to the steaming wok. "See that hot wok.? I am going to create a piece in the gallery that creates that sound and energy. The water will drip mysteriously from the ceiling and burst into steam when it hits the red-hot wok. I am going to call it Fire and Rain."

Nomo looked up and down Canal Street, stared up at the sky, and responded, "Far fucking out.

Okay, my turn. Come with me."

They continued walking along Canal Street until they came to a sidewalk fish market with an ancient awning with illegible printing. The pungent smell reached deep into the nostrils and went right down to the shoes. Nomo was staring at the tank of lobsters.

Qwerty told the cranky Chinese fish salesman, "That lobster is dead."

The Chinese fish salesman reached into the tank, grabbed a lobster, shook it in the air, flailing its claws up and down, and shouted, "Look. Alive, alive!"

Nomo looked at Qwerty and laughed. "Alive, alive, okay!"

Nomo took out his camera. "Walk up to the basket of crabs and pull one out. Act like a customer, then run down the street with the crab. I follow you and film you and the guys at the market chasing you."

"Okay, Q-man, action!"

Nomo stood on the sidewalk nearby and began filming the scene. In the front of the stand, there was a basket of blue crabs. One large and colorful crab was climbing up the side and was about halfway over the edge. Qwerty began the performance by running to the basket, reaching down and grabbing the crab firmly in his hand. He waved the crab at the market workers under the awning and yelled, "Free the blue crabs! Free blue crabs!"

He then started running west on Canal Street toward the Hudson River. Two Chinese market workers ran after him, and Nomo took it all in on camera. The workers soon realized they might be crazy and returned to the stand. When Qwerty and Nomo reached the Hudson, they crossed under the West Side Highway to an abandoned pier. Qwerty created an elaborate ceremony in which he had a three-way conversation with himself, the crab, and the gods. Nomo recorded the entire ceremony and saved Qwerty's performance for history. They laughed and danced around all the way back to Qwerty's apartment on Sullivan Street.

"That was a blast, Nomo. We may start a new movement to return seafood to the oceans."

"First, someone will have to save me from my landlord and from being evicted," Nomo said before breaking out in laughter.

"So, Nomo, what did you think of my idea for the piece? The wok and the steam captivated my attention. The idea of fire and rain connecting us to that other world just raced through my mind. I was thinking of using bigger pieces of steel and more fire in other pieces," Qwerty said.

"Man, you are going to need a big studio." Nomo replied.

The Hell's Angels were gathering at the bar on Bleecker Street, and they could hear the racket and smell the pot. It invited them to go down to the streets and look for mischief. It was a good time to be young and free.

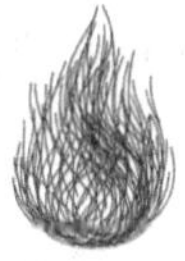

CHAPTER EIGHT

Showtime

June is the beginning of summer for the art world. Art dealers prepare to hibernate and enjoy summer activities out of town. It is a time for Maine, beach houses in the Hamptons, or share the previous season's art with the summer venues in the far-flung countryside.

Qwerty stood inside the Green Gallery on a June Sunday morning, facing the pristine white space in the back room, contemplating his installation. The image of the clouds of steam and smoke in the store window kitchen began to take epic proportions in his mind. That process is familiar to most artists. An artist can't complete a piece in the studio until the idea is unbearably epic. The process reverses itself after the piece is completed.

He had modified his wok and added a stainless-steel strainer to house the burner. Under that set a propane burner that he had found in a surplus store on Canal Street. Canal Street was lined with stores providing an endless supply of surplus material no longer used in industry. These stores were a resource for artists to find objects for their work and their living spaces. The finishing touch was the placement of stones on the floor around the strainer. The stones added a reference to Mother Earth. The water drip from the ceiling was fed by plastic tubing that snaked above the ceiling. The small battery-operated water pump was behind the wall connected to the tubing. The pump was also a find from a Canal Street surplus supply. He had modified an aquarium bubbler to send just enough water to drip from a funnel at the ceiling. He turned the valve on the propane tank and fired up the burner. Next, he started his water pump. To his amazement, it worked. At first, the water collected in the wok, but after wiping it up and heating the wok, it fell in drops that exploded into steam.

The gallery owners expected some candles, so he prepared sixteen triangular shelves, installed them in the corner of the alcove leading to the back room, and placed beeswax candles in glass cups on each. He felt relieved when all the candles were lit, and the wok was fired up. The final step was to take a series of slides with his trusty Pentax camera. Slides were the currency of artist-to-market communications, a lesson he had learned from working at the gallery. When He finished his work, Qwerty sat in a director's chair and savored the moment. Somehow, this was the reward he needed most from his work and newfound profession. He didn't think much about his identity as an artist or how he became one. He was learning that if he just followed the path before him, he would experience the life that was meant to be.

The moment had arrived for the gallery to open. A table with wine for the patrons was set up in the reception area, and the elevator was unlocked to let the opening begin.

Thursday evenings on Madison Avenue and 57th Street in New York City belonged to the art world. Most galleries reserved this night at least once a month for opening new exhibitions. This Thursday marked the introduction of Qwerty Blanc.

The exhibition was installed, the work was lit, the wine bar was set up, and the patrons came through the door. The eclectic mix of gallery patrons was divided into three groups. One group was quite elegant, with men in tuxedos and ladies wearing jewelry reserved for special occasions. This group usually dressed for whatever else the evening offered after the opening. Lincoln Center events were well-timed for post-gallery shows. The second group was dressed in a wardrobe that always stayed the same from their daily life except for an occasional cleaning. The third group included people who were dressed especially for art openings. Their outfits represented the real avant-garde fashion statement. They were clean and pressed and dressed to impress. All groups were represented at the opening that night.

Richard arrived and entered the back room. He stood silent for a long time before pacing about and exiting without saying a word. Qwerty assumed that he was disappointed in the work or just not impressed. Qwerty walked to the reception area for a glass of wine.

Richard was talking to a distinguished-looking group of people who had just arrived.

Richard addressed the group, "When we go to the back room, please just stand for a moment in silence and experience the work with all your senses. I think you will agree that this work is truly new and important." Qwerty was stunned.

Nomo was chatting with a young woman dressed in jeans and a bit disheveled. Qwerty had seen her at the gallery openings several times. She worked for the Village Voice newspaper. Most articles in the Village Voice were focused on issues that other newspapers avoid. The writers were keenly interested in matters that directly affected the counterculture living in Greenwich Village. Qwerty read every issue of the paper. One of the many revelations for him was that being gay in New York was illegal. Gay people seemed quite normal and certainly not illegal. The Village Voice was advocating change in the law and the attitude of its readers. The paper also closely followed trends in music and art. Qwerty was happy to see someone from the Village Voice at the show that day.

Nomo introduced the young woman.

" This is F.J."

Qwerty smiled and said, "Glad you could come to the show. My pieces are in the back room."

"They caught my attention. The use of flames in your work sends a message to young artists to burn down old and tired ideas in art. When I saw the steam rising into the air, I felt the spirit of the piece had reached out to greet me. Nice work."

Qwerty was stunned that his work communicated something profound. His response was simply, "Wow. Thanks."

As she walked away, she said, "Looking forward to seeing more of your work in the future."

Nomo looked at Qwerty with a grin. "Q-man, your work is scorching -ha ha."

"Yeh, well, she thought my work was cool," Qwerty replied with a wink.

There was a lot of activity in and out of the conference room. Few collectors seemed to be spending time there, but he recognized some other gallery and museum types and engaged in lively conversation with Richard and his silent partner.

As the event ended, Richard approached Qwerty and said, "I have good news. The Whitney Museum wants to put your fire and rain sculpture in their next annual exhibition of contemporary American sculpture. These annual shows are becoming increasingly relevant to introducing people to new artists here in New York. Congratulations."

Qwerty asked, "Are you sure?'

Richard smiled and said, "They didn't hesitate. Don't expect a raise just because you are now officially an artist in this gallery."

Qwerty was the last person to leave. He shut down his pieces, put away the wine bar, and checked the rooms for stragglers. He felt content as he turned off the lights. His next stop would be Fanelli's Bar, where he would treat himself to a shot of whiskey and a draft beer chaser.

Fanelli's was business as usual, dark and welcoming. Sitting at the bar was an artist who was a frequent visitor to the gallery. They chatted for a time and became familiar with each other. Qwerty knew that he was a painter but nothing about the paintings themselves. His name was Alan, and he seemed full of himself. Alan had mentioned that he lived in a loft in SoHo. He seemed to know everything going on in SoHo's fledging world of art.

"What's it like living and having a studio in a SoHo loft?" Qwerty asked.

"The zoning in SoHo is called commercial and not residential. Artists play hide and seek with the building department since we technically aren't supposed to live in commercial lofts."

Qwerty asked, "Aren't you afraid you will get in trouble?"

"It's worth it because we can get great big studios with cheap rent. The businesses are leaving, and landlords need to rent the space. They don't care what we do, and technically, we are manufacturing something."

Qwerty said with a smile, "We are manufacturing art. Never thought of it that way."

"I am heading there now if you want to see for yourself," Alan replied, adjusting the cash left on the bar.

Alan's loft was on Broome Street. The facade was typical of the classic cast iron buildings in SoHo. The facade was composed of a series of cast iron Greco-Roman columns arranged evenly from one side to the other on the street elevation. The entry door opened to a dingy lobby composed of an entry to a freight elevator and a six-foot-wide staircase that ascended uninterrupted for three stories. They walked up two flights of stairs to a metal-clad door that opened into the open space with walls and a ceiling covered in peeling paint. The coating was a water-based calcium-based material used in the original construction. The walls were constructed with the horsehair-reinforced plaster applied to the wood lath. There were no original interior walls except for the two bathrooms located in the front corner by the elevator shaft. In the center was a strange structure that resembled cabin walls covered in four-millimeter clear polyethylene plastic sheeting.

Alan had constructed some gypsum walls with track lighting to hang his large white paintings. His paintings were much larger than Qwerty was used to seeing. He thought their scale was responding to Alan's bigger-than-life studio space. At first, the paintings appeared to be just plain white, but color magically appeared in subtle geometric variations. The effect captivated Qwerty. The subtle color variations seemed to vibrate, which gave the surface an incredible energy.

"Alan, where do you sleep?" was the first thing Qwerty could think of to say.

Alan replied by pointing to the structure in the center of the space. He parted the plastic, and they entered a cozy little home that resembled a one-room cabin. There was a bedroom and living area with throw rugs and bookshelves.

"The zoning considers my studio residence illegal. I hide my living area in case an inspector comes by. The landlords just need rent, so they don't care. These spaces are emptying out fast."

"Far out!" Qwerty said, "Artists are meant to be outlaws."

"Never thought of it that way but it does kind of fit."

"Any shows coming up for your work?"

"A vacant building on Greene Street just south of Prince Street became available for artists to use for an exhibition space this week. The owner's son is an artist. Somehow, he persuaded his father to let him use the storefront for a temporary exhibit. I was invited to hang a painting; perhaps you could join in the fun." Alan said.

"Thanks for the invitation, Alan. Just let me know the details and I will be there. It has been a long day, so I am going to hit the sack. Thanks for the tour." Qwerty said as he opened the oversized steel door to the staircase.

CHAPTER NINE

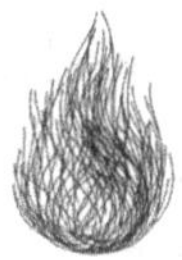

Somebody Call the Fire Department

The show at the Green Gallery was well received. Richard told Qwerty that his future as an artist looked bright, but it would be a long time before he could expect to make a living selling his artwork. Qwerty thought he could always have gallery work to support himself and had never considered the prospect of making money from his art. He enjoyed working at an art gallery, but there were times that he thought his nickname might become "fetch."

A few days later, Qwerty met Alan at the Greene Street building. The building had a typical cast iron façade like Alan's building on Broome Street. It had been vacant for some time. The area was preparing for the Lower Manhattan Expressway. SoHo was about to disappear as a loft manufacturing district. Opposition to destroying the unique architecture and character of the neighborhood was growing, but the future was uncertain.

Qwerty was fascinated by the energy in the pop-up shows in SoHo. "Happening "was the moniker Claus had coined.

The enormous storefront space was theatrical, with a twenty-foot ceiling height and no interior walls. Nature abhors a vacuum, so artists felt compelled to fill the entire space. The floors were wood, resembling an old barn floor. The space was dark except for some skylights at the rear. Most artists brought clamp lights from their studios. Fortunately, the electric service was still working.

Qwerty found an area that looked promising for setting up artwork. An artist was busy placing a large, galvanized steel pan on the floor next to the space. Qwerty had recently seen the artist at the Green Gallery but didn't know his name.

He said to Qwerty. "I saw your piece at the last happening. Are you going to do something like that?"

"There are no rules, right? I want to use melted beeswax about an inch thick in the center of a circular pan and a lighted wick in the middle. The yellow color of beeswax is amazing, and the candlelight in the middle should really make it glow."

"Right on! I am doing this large metal pan containing turpentine mixed with black oil paint with an easel in the middle. The color of the liquid is jet black, with a nice reflection of the easel. The smell of the turpentine reminds me of being in a painter's studio." Dennis replied.

"It stinks," Qwerty said. "Just kidding. I think the piece is cool."

They agreed to meet at the opening. His experience with Claus at the last pop-up show was fun, and he looked forward to this one.

The artists completed their work a few days later, and it was showtime. The opening was packed with young artists and their friends. There were also established artists, art professors, and a new group of gallery owners. The atmosphere was electric, and patrons were rapidly moving about. Qwerty worried his piece wouldn't stay lit. He made some last-minute adjustments to the size of the wick in the center. The large crowd was making Qwerty nervous. People were walking and standing too close to the work on the floor. People were smoking and drinking and crowding the artwork. Suddenly, someone stepped on the edge of the pan next to Qwerty's work containing the turpentine and paint mixture, and it ran over onto the old wood floor. The mixture burst into flames when it reached Qwerty's giant beeswax candle piece.

Panic set in, and people started yelling and running for the front door since it was the only way out. The flames spread quickly and continued until some of the sprinkler heads finally burst open with water. Fortunately, the building had a working sprinkler system with an alarm that alerted the Fire Department. In a matter of minutes, the street was filled with first responders.

The firemen set to work and started helping people with burns and injuries who had been injured in the stampede to the exit. When the fire was extinguished, there was a large crowd in the streets, and the press arrived to report on the disaster. The New York Post and Daily News loved disasters, and they were some of the first to arrive.

The fire made the front page of both the Post and the News, and suddenly, Qwerty was notorious. No one mentioned that the turpentine piece caught fire and was the reason for the rapid spread of the flames. The press focused on the artist known for using fire in his art. Qwerty was an easy target. The Post and the Daily News had no interest in confusing their readers.

Fortunately, no one died. Most injuries occurred in the panic to exit. The fire was contained to the store level and the rest of the building was not involved in the flames. This type of old cast iron building would have become a fire trap were it not for the sprinkler system and strict compliance. The art world owed its new home to the poor souls who lost their lives in the Triangle Shirtwaist Company fire of 1911. Artists could now inhabit and work in these spaces without becoming toast. The mandated sprinkler systems made SoHo a safe haven for artist's studios.

When Qwerty returned to his apartment on Sullivan Street, he sat in the darkness, wondering how he could face the world again in New York City. The Greene Street fire suddenly turned his world upside down. He had never experienced notoriety before. He enjoyed the attention he received at the Green Gallery show but now felt the need to hide.

Summer meant a break in his usual routine. He decided that since the gallery was closing for the season, it might be a good time to return upstate and spend the summer with Alice and Adam. Much of his spare time was spent visiting museums and reading art history books. He was especially interested in the likes of Clement Greenburg to understand post-World War II American Art. He loved the glorious color and grand scale of Barnet Newman and Mark Rothko. His personal favorite was Jackson Pollack. He would walk down the streets of the Village and imagine Pollack throwing paint every which way with a cigarette still clinging to his lips, turning intellectuals into rock and roll fans. The whole system of Modern Art seemed to be populated with Mad Hatters, and Qwerty loved them all. He was terrified that the building fire might put an end to him being a part of his new-found world. It was time to pause.

He packed his belongings to empty the apartment on Sullivan Street in the Village. Adam Deedle drove his pick-up truck down to New York City to return him to the farm. Adam was usually a good driver but driving in New York City traffic made him panic. He was parked in the opposite direction of traffic on Sullivan Street. When Qwerty saw the truck parked opposite traffic, he decided to drive Adam home.

As they entered the Lincoln tunnel on their way to the Thruway and home, Qwerty turned to Adam and said, "Thanks for coming to get me. I realize that driving in New York City is no fun."

"Seems like everyone here is in a gosh darn hurry!"

Adam spent most of the trip quietly observing the countryside along the Thruway. They didn't talk much on the trip, and Adam wasn't much on small talk anyway. There was no mention of the fire, and Qwerty understood that he needed to keep his new career to himself. Alice and Adam would not understand the world of art, and there was no need to confuse them with his new identity as an artist. This was a time for Qwerty to lay low.

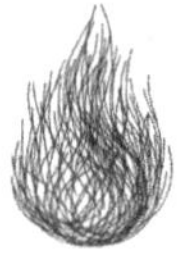

Chapter Ten

The Draft

The pop-up show fire received a great deal of attention in the New York newspapers. The fire became a magnet for criticism of the arts, the safety of SoHo buildings, and especially allowing people to assemble without a proper permit. Qwerty's name was frequently mentioned throughout the entire news cycle. His notoriety faded, as did fame from news events in New York. The art world, however, turned his brief notoriety into legend. Qwerty was unaware of the positive effect of his notoriety. He believed his new career was over.

"Welcome back to being Hank Smith," he mused. He was content that he could leave the confusion he felt behind him. It was time to return to the comfort of Hank Smith's world.

He settled in at the farmhouse and resumed his life as Hank. Alice made sandwiches for lunch and fine home-cooked dinners.

Her life was full, as she continued to work as the Town Clerk and to volunteer at the church, but she missed Hank dearly. Adam returned to the fields. He was happy to return to brush-hogging the pastures. Hank found his flyrod, net and creel in the back entry. He returned to the river to find the peaceful sport trout fishing provided.

Alice called for supper as the sun descended over the mountain to the west.

"There is no sweeter sound on this earth than Alice calling us," Hank said to some trout wiggling in his creel.

"God, I love that sound," Adam said to his tractor.

"Why do I always have to call those boys for supper? They know what time it is." Alice said to herself, wiping her hands on her apron.

Hank and Adam were washing up in the mudroom when Adam started clearing his throat. Over the years, Hank recognized this sound as a warning that Adam had something on his mind.

"Got some sad news, Hank." Adam looked down with sadness in his eyes and continued, "Andy Brucher from your high school class was killed in Vietnam. The Board of Supervisors is going to name a road for him. That's nice but that ain't going to bring Sarah and George's boy back to them." Adam looked around, wiping his lips on a napkin. "Are you against this war like some of them college kids are? Heck, they keep saying it's not a war and say that our soldiers are just advising the government there in Vietnam fighting commies."

Hank responded, "I haven't been paying much attention to the news. I don't have a TV, and my life in the city has been full of new adventures. I don't even know where my draft card is. I thought we were worried about atomic bombs and the Russians, not rice farmers in Vietnam."

"I was the same way when I was your age, and then one day, ended up in Korea," Adam said, taking off one of his boots. "See them missing toes? Frostbite. The Army doctors had to take 'em off."

After a brief pause, Adam continued, "I was just north of the DMZ in a small bunker with my buddy John Jones. He was from Texas, Wichita Falls, I think. Anyway, me and Jones was in this outpost one night and it was freakin cold. There wasn't much going on. They said the Chinese were joining in a counteroffensive soon. We didn't see nothin' so we were smokin' and jokin'. All of a sudden, all hell broke loose. There were machine gun tracers flying over us and noise you wouldn't believe. A fifty-caliber machine gun tracer come at me and glanced off the top of my helmet. Knocked me out cold. I woke up when some gook ran over my body, passing through. My face was covered in blood. Guess they figured I was dead. Poor Jones was lying on top of my leg, deader than a doornail. I passed out and woke up in a hospital with my head and one foot bandaged. Frost bite took them toes. Poor Jones kept my other foot from freezing. Fortunately, I only suffered a mild concussion from the helmet being struck."

Adam paused momentarily, then continued, "Hank, it wasn't like returning from World War II. We didn't get no parades because we didn't win. I never felt the same about this country. You are a man now and you may have to serve your country. Right or wrong, a man must do these things. This Vietnam business sounds just like Korea. Wouldn't surprise me if it ended up the same way."

Hank realized he never got to know his adopted father. All the years came and went without establishing a true bond. He was stunned by what Adam had told him. He had never been able to communicate well with Adam except to learn the skills necessary to build and manage the farm. Adam understood nature and how things worked, but interacting with people was a mystery. Alice was all about getting along with people and her community. Hank was a product of the two personalities.

The summer passed quickly. There was time to work on the farm, go fly fishing on the Battenkill, and catch up on reading. Bertrand Russell and Carl Jung broadened his horizons and understanding of the visual arts. Reading the essays by Clement Greenberg gave him a better understanding of the abstract expressionists and the state of art in New York City. He was reading about the history of visual arts and realized that he was living in a period of significant changes for the future. He remembered Richard referring to Prometheus one day at the gallery after the opening. He decided to go to the local library to learn more about the Greek God Prometheus and the gift of fire. He wondered if the story had something to do with his new career. The problem with Greek mythology for him was that it seemed a bit more complicated than he could wrap his mind around. He concluded that inspiration should remain a mystery.

One September evening, Adam and Hank were enjoying an apple pie dessert that Alice had prepared. After they finished and gave Alice sufficient praise for her apple pie, Adam handed Hank official letters from the Draft Board.

"You weren't at the Post Office with me, so I signed for 'em," Adam said.

Hank was mortified. "Why did you sign for these?" Hank asked.

"They looked important," Adam responded.

"Yeah, sure, important. One letter is for me to report for a physical exam; the other is a notice to report for the draft into the Army. It looks like I am off to Vietnam. Thanks a lot." Hank shot back to Adam while pacing back and forth by the table.

Alice added, "Now Hank, we owe it to our country and our community to serve when we are called upon. I want to be proud of you. And don't you talk to Adam that way."

"Ain't so sure about what we owe our country, Alice," Adam said quietly.

Alice continued, "I was reading in the paper just the other day about your friend Bernie from your high school baseball team. Seems he left for Canada to avoid the draft. They even had a picture of him in an office in Toronto that helps other American boys who want to go to Canada to avoid the draft. I am telling you; it was all the talk at the Chit Chat Café."

"Bernie is a good friend, and I am sure he had good reason," Hank said.

"I am sure he did, but we don't do things like that around here, young man," Alice said sternly as she cleared the table and retired to the kitchen.

The draft notice left Hank numb. After dinner, he went to his room to read. He was determined to learn as much as he could about art and try to understand why he was so absorbed by it. He decided to spend the days that he remained on the farm reading and enjoying the beauty of the river.

On a bright fall morning, Hank drove Alice to Fort Hamilton in Brooklyn for his physical. Worrying about Alice's safe return upstate distracted him from his situation.

The Army base hospital at Fort Hamilton was large, but the entrance to the clinic set up for draft physicals was easy to see. Quietly, the draft had expanded to the point that quite a large crowd was entering for physicals. Hank secretly hoped they would find something wrong and reject him.

After filling out all the forms and parading from one medical station to the next in his underwear, he stood at the table where a doctor reviewed his exam results.

"You have a heart murmur," the doctor said. Hank was feeling a sigh of relief when the doctor added. "It's probably just functional." The doctor stamped "PASSED" as Hank stood in disbelief.

He returned to the farm by train. As he enjoyed the scenic views of the Hudson from the train window, his mind wandered through the events of the past few years. Hank contemplated being taken from his adventures in New York City, back to his life on the farm, and to yet another life where he would soon become government property for two years.

The leaves were turning magical colors and beginning to fall as Alice drove him to Whitehall Street in lower Manhattan. "I am proud of you, Hank. Adam and I will be thinking about you every day.

I packed a sandwich and some apple pie."

"Not to worry, everything is going to be fine. I am going to miss your apple pie. There is a city deli with a sign that says to send a salami to your boy in the Army. Isn't that funny?"

Alice started to cry, signaling Hank to go inside with one final kiss goodbye.

The Whitehall Street Induction Center was a modest place for a famous induction center. The center was a series of office spaces with standard fluorescent lighting and modest furnishings. He took a series of written tests and, at the end of the day, was escorted into a room with other inductees to be sworn in. He raised his right hand, swore to protect and defend the Constitution, and suddenly became Private Hank Smith United States Army. After a short subway ride with his group, they arrived at Penn Station to board a train to Washington, D.C. After arriving in Washington, they changed trains to another southbound train bound for Fort Jackson, South Carolina. This train was the Rock Island Line. Hank was familiar with the name from the old-time country song of the same name.

Hank had never been in the South and the train ride was a culture shock. The sleeper train was local and stopped at sections of the towns and cities that were segregated for blacks. The houses in his hometown were old, but the people along the tracks lived in shacks. The porters and train workers were black and spoke to him with a drawl and strange politeness that seemed condescending in reverse. As the day ended, he climbed into his sleeping cubby for the night and drifted off to sleep as the train chattered down the tracks. With the motion, he dreamed he was driving a car at night, and the lights went out. He tried to slam on the brakes and there were none. He started screaming. The train porter awakened him.

"How y'all doing, sir?" asked the old porter with a smile.

"I'm okay. Thanks," Hank said, but he knew he wasn't okay at all. The dream was a sign that he had no control over his future.

The next day, they arrived at the makeshift Reception Center at Fort Jackson. Young soldiers wearing black armbands with temporary corporal strips hustled Hank and the recruits off the train. They yelled obscenities constantly and referred to the new arrivals as Joe.

"Hey, Joe. Jody got your girl, Jody got your car, and you are here in the Army now." was a refrain repeated by the acting corporals that herded the inductees about at the processing center. The new arrivals were given ponchos to wear even though the weather was sunny. This was someone's idea of a temporary uniform. Eventually, they were given haircuts, real uniforms and vaccinations before being assigned to tents for the night. After a few days of processing, Hank was assigned to a basic training unit and moved into a barracks building. He was lucky to get one of the old barracks since many new arrivals were housed in tents. The draft had expanded the recruitment to overflowing. A low-hanging cloud of coal smoke was present early in the morning when they assembled in platoons for reveille. Coal was the heating fuel of the South and was unpleasant compared to the wood smoke of the homes in the North.

Processing was completed two days later, and drill sergeants escorted the recruits to their basic training unit. The atmosphere changed dramatically as the recruits were introduced to professional soldiers who would train them. They were organized into squads, platoons and a company. Some harassment and abuse continued, but the atmosphere became professional. After settling into the assigned barracks, they were introduced to their drill sergeants. Drill sergeants wore an impressive flat-brimmed hat that resembled the hat that Smoky the Bear wore. They ruled the roost in basic training.

Sergeant Hyers, an impressive first-class sergeant, was in charge of Hank's platoon. He stood six feet tall and resembled the actor Randolph Scott from the golden age of movies. He asked Hank where he was from. When Hank said he was from New York, he grinned and said, "We don't like people from New York down here. I am going to make you a squad leader since you think you are smarter than us hicks." A squad was a seven-man subdivision of the platoon of about forty soldiers. He stood Hank at the beginning of the first line of the platoon formation. Hank's assignment was to count the number of men in his squad and call out that number when the drill sergeant said "report." At six o'clock in the morning, the reveille formation was set, a cannon fired in the distance, and a bugle sounded over loudspeakers. The drill sergeants saluted and then did snappy about-faces.

"Report," Hyers sounded to his new platoon.

Hank replied, "About seven."

Hyers walked directly in front of Hank until the bill of his hat hit his forehead and said, "I don't want to know ABOUT! I want to know exactly, trainee."

All Hank could see were two rows of perfect and magnificent teeth. "Yes! drill sergeant!"

Hank thought to himself that the next two years would be long ones. Despite all the nonsense, Hank found all this to be a kind of theater. He would learn his part and join in the play. His basic training passed quickly. It was Christmas and the Army treated the graduates to a free plane ride from Colombia, South Carolina, to their home cities. Hank had never been on a plane before and hadn't seen a female in ten weeks. The airlines chose the stewardesses for their youthful good looks and sex appeal. This was not lost on the recruits who had been sequestered in training for two months.

The plane arrived at Newark Airport. Hank was able to take a bus to the Port Authority Bus Terminal in Manhattan and then board another bus to Albany. Alice and Adam were happy to see him when they picked him up at the bus station.

"What a great Christmas present!" Alice said as Hank loaded his duffle bag into their pickup truck.

"What's next, Hank?" Adam asked.

"I am going Fort Benning for what is called Advanced Infantry Training. After the training, I will join an infantry unit in Vietnam."

"Let's enjoy this time we have together. We will be worried about you every day when you are gone. Please write to us often so that we know you are okay." Alice said while reaching out for Hank's hand.

"It's okay, Alice. I am going to be fine," Hank said, turning to Alice.

Hank spent the two weeks at home enjoying the holiday celebrations with childhood friends and neighbors. Alice's cooking really shined during the holiday season. The two weeks passed quickly.

When Hank arrived at Fort Benning to complete his infantry training, he began to doubt why he hadn't gone to Canada as his friend Bernie had done. Hank thought the war represented the worst of America but couldn't resolve the idea of shaming Alice and his hometown. He admired Bernie's integrity and commitment to standing against the war. When a boy was raised in a small town in America during the fifties, there was a tendency to want to be either a cowboy or a soldier. The fantasies were inescapable. Little did they realize that fantasies can become nightmares.

Infantry training was a form of theater for Hank. The training required Hank to use the incredible variety of weapons used by the infantry. There were rifles, machine guns, mortars, and even anti-tank weapons. Since the weapons were used in theatrical ranges, there was no reality of their deadly potential. Blowing targets apart was not that much different from the fireworks he played with as a boy. He especially liked firing the fifty-caliber machine gun and hand-held anti-tank weapons at old steel wrecks on the ranges. The shouts of kill, kill, kill during bayonet training were more macabre theater. For some reason, he and the other trainees never realized that the words were meant to be used in battle to kill the enemy. The commandment to not kill was etched in his mind as a child but suddenly thou shalt kill an enemy was sanctioned.

It was there that he met Jimmy Meyers. Jimmy was a redheaded boy drafted while he was an art student at Pratt Institute in Brooklyn. Jimmy had no illusions about what they were being trained to do. He railed against the war, racism, and the corruption of the military-industrial complex. The common ground was their interest in the arts. They shared books and conversations about the evolution of man through the arts. Hank asked Jimmy what he would do when they got to Vietnam. Jimmy responded that he was going to be a medic. He said he couldn't change his situation other than to try and do something good in all that mess.

As the training ended, the graduates were being processed for orders to their units in Vietnam. Hank and Jimmy found themselves with time on their hands.

Hank said, "Let's play some pool."

Jimmy said," I'm just too damn good at pool to play with you."

"Bullshit," Hank said as he racked the pool balls for a game of eight balls.

Jimmy ran the entire field and promptly sank the eight ball. Hank was dumbstruck. He suggested they go to the next company and make a few bucks.

Gambling was common in the barracks. There was a feeling that there was nothing to lose since they were all headed for destruction. When they got to the dayroom in the next company, there was a poker game and betting at the pool table. Jimmy signed up for pool and was winning quite a bit of money. The losers were not pleased.

Hank sat at the poker table. They played for an hour until a pot at Hank's table was hundreds of dollars. Even though the bets started at a few dollars, there was no limit. Hank had three of a kind and drew a pair. He went all in. He collected the pot and got up from the table. Jimmy saw what had happened and did an incredible trick shot at the pool table.

They calmly walked out the door. Realizing the losers might beat them up, they both ran for their lives. They hid under their barracks and eventually laughed when the coast was clear. They realized that they had just established an unbreakable bond with each other.

The orders for unit assignments were posted on the company bulletin board. Jimmy got his wish and was assigned as a medic. Hank was a garden variety grunt assigned to the First Calvary. They had a few days to go to Atlanta and enjoy their easy money. They spent some time in a hotel on Peachtree Street until it was time to return to the base to board their plane for Vietnam.

The flight was long and tedious, with a quick layover in Hawaii. The trip to Vietnam was by Army transport. When the plane landed, Hank dragged his duffle bag off the loading dock and joined the line formed for First Calvary arrivals. He and Jimmy were unceremoniously separated. Hank waved goodbye to Jimmy and wondered if he would ever see his buddy again.

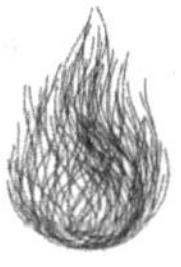

CHAPTER ELEVEN

Nam

The Air Force base near Saigon was a vast area of supplies, equipment and groups of uniformed soldiers as far as the eye could see. After processing in a trailer near the landing area, he was ordered to join the First Calvary Division. The First Calvary insignia was larger than most and had a bold yellow and black design. The First Calvary was no longer a calvary in the sense of horses and riders. The childhood fantasies of playing cowboys and Indians, with the cavalry coming to the rescue, were replaced by reality. This cavalry was a specialized military unit focused on deploying troop-carrying helicopters quickly, facing constant danger. He liked the design of the patch for his uniform but didn't know much about the unit or his destination.

In addition to the new arrivals, there were the departing troops. The new arrivals had dark green fatigue uniforms and duffle bags that still smelled of storage. The departing soldiers were a rag-tag bunch. They were sullen and messy. These boys were men now and seemed to bear the weight of their experience. They were battle-weary. Hank thought that they should be happy to be going home. They had served their country and were returning to their girlfriends and family. Their hometowns should welcome them with open arms. Little did he know, their homecoming was far from the warm reception he had anticipated.

The next few weeks were spent at orientations. The next stop was a bus ride to a headquarters unit. The First Calvary was part of the new style of infantry delivered by helicopter. They would go to an objective by air, drop off the infantry and return after wreaking havoc. There didn't seem to be a real objective to the operation. After the final orientation and paperwork, he climbed into a Chinook helicopter to join his unit in the field. The Chinook helicopter was large and loud, designed to carry a platoon of troops. When they approached the landing site, Hank could see a large gathering of tents, troops milling about and a few smaller helicopters on small fields. As the group departed the helicopter, they walked to one of the tents with a yellow flag and a black horse head. Standing by the entrance was the one and only Sergeant Howard Hyers.

"I never thought I would see you here!" Hank shouted.

"It wasn't my idea. I've got nineteen years in this man's Army and will retire after this tour."

Hank was surprised to be greeted by his old basic training drill sergeant. He had admired him and was glad to see a familiar face. He knew he was in good hands with him as his platoon sergeant here. It didn't take long to see the change in him now that his job was in a war zone. His fierce blue eyes were now sincere and sympathetic. Hank wondered if the career soldiers believed in this conflict. This platoon sergeant was a consummate professional. There was no doubt he would have preferred to stay at Fort Jackson or perhaps a tour in Germany.

"Well, I'll be damned!" Qwerty said.

"Look what the cat dragged in. Hey, city kid. It looks like we're stuck with each other," Hyers replied.

"Sergeant, I hate to admit it, but I admire you."

"Thanks, kid. I didn't want any part of this, but I had no choice with two years left before my retirement. This thing is out of control and some of the best people I know are getting out to keep from coming back here. It is destroying the army that I love."

"I am just a draftee, so I never thought of that."

"Well, let's just go do what we got to do son."

Hank settled in his bunk. The following day, Sergeant Hyers burst into the tent.

"Drop your cocks and grab your socks! Boys, we're heading to the field! Chop-chop."

Hank and his platoon scrambled to assemble their gear and boarded another Chinook helicopter on their first trip to the field. The helicopter sound made his eardrums pulse. At first, they were high above the terrain until they ascended toward a series of rice paddies. The helicopter landed on a grassy field with orange smoke flares at the perimeter. Sergeant Hyers was the first to jump out of the open door, yelling at the boys to follow him. Suddenly, there was a deafening explosion. Hank was covered in blood and pieces of uniforms and flesh. He found himself on the ground, unable to move his legs. He was clinging to his M16 rifle as he rolled toward a body lying nearby. It was Sergeant Hyers. He turned his head toward Hank and smiled with those magnificent teeth. Hank remembered how funny Sergeant Hyers was at times during basic training. He had a saying for all situations.

"A happy soldier is a busy soldier," Hank managed to say. "To be happy is to work," Hyers managed to say with some choking. Sergeant Hyers died there. He was far from his South Carolina home and his beloved family. All that humor and humanity just passed into the tropical sunshine.

Hank felt a burning pain in his back. He was surrounded by chaos and the sounds of cursing and gunfire. Slowly everything began to fade away. He thought this was the end. That is all there is. Life was not supposed to be this short. The sunshine cooled, and his sight went black.

That was Hank's last memory as he regained consciousness a week later in a hospital at Fort Dix in New Jersey. He had been airlifted to McGuire Air Force Base from a hospital in Vietnam.

Alice and Adam Deedle were sitting at his bedside.

"We didn't think you were going to make it, buddy," Adam said.

Alice wiped the tears from her eyes. "I love you Hank and I hate this damn war."

A lieutenant came into the room. "Payday Private Smith, sign here." The officer said.

"What happened to my unit, sir?" Hank asked.

"Your helicopter was hit by mortar fire and overrun by North Vietnamese Regulars. You are the only survivor. You have spinal injuries."

Hank thought of Sergeant Hyers and the boys he had met who were never coming home to their families. A happy soldier is a busy soldier. Bullshit. He found solace in reading about art and history, but months passed before he could return to anything resembling normal.

Hank spent the remainder of his Army service convalescing at what was called Headquarters Company at Fort Dix. The returnees in that company seemed lost and confused, without much concern for anything other than returning to their home streets. Much of Hank's remaining time was spent in physical therapy.

Hank helped pass the time in the headquarters company office. The company clerk, Phil, was a pleasant former trainee who was held over at Fort Dix because he claimed to be a conscientious objector. He had made that decision after being drafted. He was making his case on religious grounds as a devout Catholic. The government didn't support the idea that Catholics could claim a religious conscientious objection to the war. It appeared that Phil would get no support from his church either. Radical priests were joining the newly forming anti-war movement, but mainstream Catholics seemed indifferent or even took a position for the war. The church itself had no official position, leaving Phil on his own. The army command at Fort Dix avoided the conflict by simply holding Phil over and giving him a job as a clerk.

One day, Phil and Hank were processing paperwork together.

Hank asked, "Phil, are you happy to avoid going to Vietnam?"

"I can't participate in the Army anymore," he said.

"Hey, you are lucky. Isn't it enough to just sit this thing out?"

"They are going to court martial me because they claim that there is no such thing as a Catholic conscientious objector. I have found a lawyer from Philadelphia to represent me. How about that? A Philadelphia lawyer – what could go wrong?"

"I don't get it, Phil; they were willing just to let you hang here and sit things out."

"Hank, there are times that we have to stand up for what we believe, or we are no better than the evil we despise."

Hank had always gone with the flow and had no experience as the rock in the stream. He thought of Bernie and wondered if he had been a coward by going into the Amy. Even with a Purple Heart medal, he never felt like much of a hero.

In the months that followed, Phil faced a court martial and was sentenced to serve time at Fort Leavenworth despite having a lawyer from Philadelphia. Hank resolved that when Phil finished his sentence, he would face the world with courage and someday accomplish something important. It was a lesson for Hank that he would carry with him when he returned to his life as Qwerty Blanc.

Hank's time in the Army came unceremoniously to an end. He signed a few forms, and a company clerk handed him an official form, DD214, summarizing his service and indicating that he was honorably discharged. He had saved a fair amount of money and decided to catch a bus to the Port Authority in New York City.

While waiting for his bus, he read a copy of the Stars and Stripes newspaper. They published the names of the casualties from Vietnam every month in alphabetical order. He scrolled down to James Meyers, Army, Specialist 4. He envisioned an anonymous lieutenant knocking on Jimmy's parent's front door with the news.

Tears rolled down Hank's cheek. "Phil and Bernie, you are right."

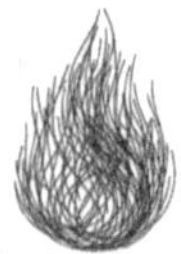

CHAPTER TWELVE

Welcome SoHo

There was a phrase used by soldiers in Vietnam called "returning to the world." Returning to the world implied that Vietnam was an alien place. The America these soldiers had left behind had changed and had become an alien place for them. There was a growing anti-war movement, and their generation was also rebelling against a culture that seemed out of touch with what they were exploring on college campuses and in urban centers. Even rock and roll music became a source of rebellion and self-evaluation. The "world," as they called it in Vietnam, was not the world that they had left behind. To make matters worse, their contemporaries treated veterans with disrespect.

Looking out the bus window on the New Jersey Turnpike, Hank decided to toss his service and upstate life out the window and onto the side of the road. He remembered the experience of leaving his upstate life behind in 1964 to become Qwerty Blanc. This return to the world would be as an artist in SoHo, resuming the career he began before the draft took him away.

As the bus entered the Lincoln Tunnel and up the maze of ramps to the Port Authority Building in Manhattan, he could feel the energy of New York City. The Port Authority Building, located near Times Square, was a place inhabited by characters that seemed to exist nowhere else in America or the planet. No one seemed to know where these characters lived, where they came from, or if they ever left Times Square once they arrived. The porn industry was given space alongside Broadway theaters. The poor and downtrodden people described at the base of the Statue of Liberty were either transformed and succeeded or still downtrodden and here.

He had been dreaming of finding a loft studio in SoHo. The draft had taken him away from his adventure as an artist. He remembered that his old friend Alan had a great loft and was a wealth of information on lofts in SoHo. After a few tries, a call to Alan went through.

"Hey Alan, it's Qwerty Blanc."

Alan seemed puzzled and said," Who? Qwerty Blanc? No way. It has been a few years, but you are a legend down here."

Qwerty was dumbfounded. "Are you kidding?"

Alan said. "The fire just added to your mystique. Photographs of your beeswax piece and the turpentine piece that caught fire were featured in ART News magazine. You both received critical praise despite the notoriety created by the press stories."

"No way!"

"Way," Alan replied.

"I just arrived in the city, and I need to find a place to live as soon as possible."

Alan hesitated momentarily and said," I have lots of room here in the loft. You could sleep on the couch and hang here until you find a place. I could use the company and you can fill me in on what you have been up to."

"Fantastic. I'll get on the subway and be there in an hour or so."

When Qwerty arrived on Broome Street, he looked around, and the buildings seemed even more deserted than when he left. He rang Alan's bell and Alan threw a sock with the door keys down to the sidewalk. He walked the grand stairway to Alan's loft. Alan was dressed in coveralls that were covered with paint. Alan had been busy stretching his large canvases with cotton duct canvas from a distributor on Walker Street onto the wooden stretchers and mixing five-gallon buckets of gesso to prime the raw canvas from Pearl Paint. Pearl Paint was located on Canal Street, at the southern border of SoHo. It was an old house paint store that the original owner's son had added an artist's supply on the second floor.

"You look busy, Alan. I'll just leave my bags and take a walk around the neighborhood."

Alan said, "That sounds good. We can get some food later and catch up. Here is a set of keys."

Qwerty decided to walk down Broadway to Murrimac Realty. Their for-sale signs were now on buildings up and down the streets of SoHo. It appeared that the entire neighborhood was on the market. Qwerty decided that he would be able to find a loft by visiting Murrimac. Their offices were on Lower Broadway just south of Canal Street. On the way, he stopped at Dave's Corner on Canal Street to sit at the counter and have lunch. The owner, Dave, of course, sat at the cash register. He reminded Qwerty of a baby bird sitting in the nest, its mouth open, begging for food. Dave was short and always seemed to have his chin pointing up when speaking to customers. He settled his check with Dave and walked two blocks further down Broadway to the Murrimac Office. Murray, Murrimac's owner, entered the office as Qwerty walked in.

"Can I help you?" he asked.

"I am looking for a loft for an art studio," Qwerty answered. He immediately realized that lofts were still illegal for artists to live in and that he might have made a mistake saying that.

Murray turned to walk toward his office and muttered, "You and every other hippie in the city." What's with the limp?"

Qwerty explained," I took some shrapnel in my back from an injury in Vietnam. It's getting better slowly but surely."

Murray hesitated and said, "Thank you for your service. We don't meet many veterans here. I hope you have some construction skills because everything we have needs a lot of work."

"That's not a problem. I am willing to renovate."

Murray said, "You may be better off looking to buy something. Everything is a fire sale around here. It's a buyer's market, for sure. Anything we have for rent is in a building that might be sold just when you finish fixing it up."

He turned away and said, "Hey, Emily, show this guy 106 Prince Street." Emily popped her head up from behind a desk partition. "Sure, okay, just a freaken minute," she said while slamming down her phone.

Emily was a robust middle-aged woman with frizzy hair and the kind of skin usually found on the beach at Coney Island on a hot summer day. She made a phone call, grabbed some keys, and motioned to Qwerty to follow her.

They walked north on Broadway to Prince Street and west to the corner of Greene Street. The building was a modest five-story brick building from the turn of the century, and it was not typical of the neighboring elegant cast iron facade buildings. The store at street level was an abandoned restaurant that had some recent fire damage. There was an active newsstand on the sidewalk, but the interior of the building was vacant. Emily waited outside while Qwerty explored. The lofts were about twenty feet wide and ninety feet long with ten-foot-high ceilings. There was light on two sides, making them ideal for studios. The fire in the restaurant had vacated the building, and only the rats remained. There wouldn't be much need for demolition, but there was an enormous amount of garbage to remove. Qwerty hadn't imagined owning a building before. The idea of ownership was intriguing, and he had savings from his two years in the Army.

Emily was standing with an old man in a disheveled dark suit, white shirt, and loose tie. He appeared to have some arthritis that caused his hands to curl and his back to be bent just below the shoulders. This man was easily a stereotype for building owners in SoHo at this time.

"I'm Dave. My brother Barry and I own this building and a few others in the neighborhood. We are in the used cardboard business on Broome Street."

Qwerty replied, "Nice to meet you, Dave. I was looking to rent a loft for a studio."

Emily said, "Look, Qwerty or whatever your name is. Just ask him how much he wants for the building. You could rent the store and a few lofts to someone else and have a loft for free."

"Okay, Emily."

Qwerty turned to Dave and asked," So, Dave, how much are you asking for the building?"

Dave said, "Thirty-five thousand dollars in cash for the building. Clean title."

"I only have about ten thousand dollars saved up from my time in the Army."

Dave looked Qwerty over, saying, "I was in the Army fighting Nazis back in the day. That was a long time ago, but I still remember. When things return to normal, people forget what you did for them. I'll tell you what I am going to do. I appreciate your service, and you seem like a nice young man. You can have the building for ten thousand down and a ten-year mortgage for the twenty-five-thousand-dollar balance."

Emily stuck her finger in the air and said, "Dave, how about five thousand down and a twenty-five-thousand-dollar mortgage for ten years?"

"You are killing me, Emily. Okay." Dave said with a grin.

Dave extended his hand to Qwerty. Qwerty had suddenly bought a loft building.

After signing a contract at the Murrimac office, Qwerty stopped at the Merchants Bank on Grand Street. Murray suggested he set up a bank account and form an LLC for the building. He set up a bank account for Qwerty and the Qwerty Blanc LLC. He transferred most of his money under Hank Smith's name from his hometown bank, which he kept as his personal account. He enjoyed having these two identities, and since his benefits went directly to the Hank Smith account, he would always have that separate bank account to fall back on.

He set to work renovating the store and cellar hoping to earn some rental income as soon as possible. He camped out on the fifth floor while he worked on the building. The removal of junk and garbage was a seemingly never-ending task. Qwerty had spent his days throwing construction debris into dumpsters that his newfound garbage expert and advisor would park at the curb on Prince Street and empty a few days later.

The debris was carted away by Dennis Bardi. He was the proud owner of Bardi Carting and a lifelong resident of Staten Island. He wore a rakish newsboy hat and knew everything you wanted to know and much more than necessary about the garbage business in New York City. Apparently, the price of garbage removal in SoHo included payments to the Mafia and various characters in the city government. Dennis was always in a hurry but always had time to tell Qwerty about another adventure in the carting business as he dropped off an empty container and picked up the full one.

Qwerty had to remove the old newsstand from the sidewalk because it didn't have a permit, and the city threatened to tax him for its use. The store had lovely tin ceilings; he had applied sheetrock to the walls and installed track lighting. Some artists he had met approached him about renting the space for a new co-op gallery. He painted the interior white and varnished the original wood floors. The co-op art gallery rented the space as soon as it was completed. He kept part of the cellar for building maintenance use and for storage. The income from the gallery rental was enough to pay the building taxes and utilities.

One sunny day, a film crew was set up to shoot a location for a TV series based in New York City. Trailers were set up along Greene Street, and delicious pastries and fruits were served to the cast and crew on the corner. The crew was busy setting up lighting, sound and cameras along the sidewalks. Qwerty always enjoyed seeing these crews and was amazed at how long it took to film a few minutes of a scene. On this day, he was working on the second floor and had just set out a small five-yard container for Dennis to pick up with his garbage truck.

Dennis had arrived and was crushing the debris from the five-yard container into the back of his garbage truck. The truck was in the street in front of the film crew's refreshment stand. Suddenly, there was a noisy commotion in the street. Qwerty immediately worried that someone from the film crew was injured.

Dennis ducked in the door and was grinning ear to ear. Dennis shrugged his shoulders and said,

"They are acting crazy out there!"

Qwerty asked, "What in the hell happened?"

A pungent, fishy odor wafted through the building, assaulting the senses with its indescribable stench. Some members of the film crew were pounding on the door as Qwerty and Dennis opened it. The garbage truck had loaded the material from the five-yard container, but some of the debris was still showing in the back compartment. The debris was coated with slime and fish parts. There was also a red-brown puddle under the back of the truck. The film crew was hastily packing up their gear and departing. Most placed handkerchiefs over their noses as they departed.

"I had a pickup at the Fulton Fish Market this morning. I figured I would add your little container as my last stop. Maybe I overdid my load. It's just some fish," Dennis said with all sincerity.

Qwerty laughed and said," I suppose that life delivers a little fish from time to time, and sometimes it smells bad. Do me a favor, Dennis, and pick my stuff up first and then go to the Fulton Fish Market."

"Peace!" Dennis said out the window of his truck, driving away.

"You stink!" Qwerty replied.

Qwerty continued working on the building and doing freelance technical work for the art galleries and dealers in SoHo. As he renovated his new studio spaces, he also began developing new artwork. He started by making variations on "Fire and Rain," adding new work using flames.

The Green Gallery was no longer in business. Richard was selling art privately with a small office on Madison Avenue. The time had come for a reunion.

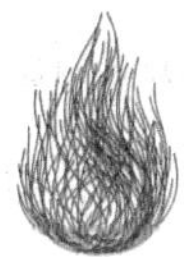

Chapter Thirteen

The Return of Qwerty Blanc

Qwerty's world revolved around his building at the corner of Prince and Greene Street. Building renovation continued, and so did the changes to the SoHo neighborhood. Paula Cooper opened a gallery two doors up on Prince Street, and there were rumors that the Reese Paley Gallery was planning to open across the street. Of course, Fanelli's Bar always had ice-cold beer only a block away. The only building that didn't change was the post office across the street. (This building was repurposed many years later to become an Apple retail outlet.)

West Broadway was a short walk from Qwerty's building. It was the main street of SoHo. Broadway was the east boundary, and Thompson Street was the west boundary. To the north, Houston Street was considered the Village and under the influence of N.Y.U.

Canal Street was considered the southern boundary, but artists were considering colonizing the area immediately below Canal Street under the moniker of Tribeca.

Most of the light manufacturing had been relocated by now, in the process of leaving, or just going out of business. The Lower Manhattan Expressway, planned for decades, was now dead in the water. This achievement was due to Jane Jacobs and other activists' intent on preserving the cast iron buildings and historic neighborhood.

The West Broadway buildings were a mix of structures with a scattering of cast iron facade and brick. 420 West Broadway was an old brick warehouse building that provided the site of one of the most consequential changes in the neighborhood. It was under construction as a gallery-building cooperative. The four gallery owners were prestigious and set the pace for additional gallery presence. This newly renovated building was the downtown location for the Leo Castelli Gallery, Sonnabend, Lawrence Rubin, and a new gallery for John Weber, the former director of the Virginia Dwan Gallery on 57 Street. Qwerty found freelance work designing and installing electrical wiring and lighting. The owners of the new galleries had more prestige than cash and always needed cheap freelance construction help.

It took the better part of a year, but finally, Qwerty substantially completed his studio building. He was busy working with steel and fire and hoped to show again. The neighborhood provided a seemingly endless source of new and interesting people. The energy was contagious. The new arrivals were interesting for a variety of reasons. The first wave was art-related, but people of all stripes followed them.

Art has a spiritual force that draws people in and turns them away. Most people revere art when they see it in museums. In the museum context, art carries with it the power of an institution. Artists and their work are met with indifference and, at times, skepticism without the support of an institution. SoHo was evolving in the space between these two extremes in the acceptance of art. The culture of SoHo allowed the idea of art having no rules as a new rule.

Qwerty spent every Saturday wandering from gallery to gallery. He would start in SoHo, then off to 57th Street, uptown to Madison Avenue, and then return to SoHo. At the end of the day, there would always be familiar faces at the Spring Street Bar to drink with and catch up on news. Art permeated his spirit, and the people who inhabited the gallery world became his tribe.

Every Saturday brought new artists and their work, but experiencing modern masters was just as exciting. Mark Rothko's color paintings and Morris Lewis's Veils, which he would see at Lawrence Rubin's gallery, saturated the depths of his mind's eye. When he saw the rusty plates of steel by Carl Andre and Richard Serra, he immediately got a powerful message.

He was fascinated with the women artists and their strange relation to organic material. He had a visceral reaction to the works of Eva Hesse. Her organic constructions of resin were organized in a disciplined and powerful way. He began to understand how abstract expressionists and artists like Eva Hesse saw structure, where others saw chaos. Qwerty had started a journey with no return ticket. He was an artist now. Living and art became one and the same.

The studio building was beginning to bear fruit. He created a workshop on the second floor. The third floor was an exhibition space so that he could better understand how the work would function in a gallery. The fourth floor was his personal gallery and storage. He reserved the fifth floor for his living space. His living space had a fireplace, skylight, a full bathroom with a sauna, and an oversized tub. He had collected used wooden pallets from the streets to reuse the wood to create a deck on the roof, which served as a micro-resort.

When the building department issued a certificate of occupancy for his building, he proudly put a small sign by the entrance that said A.I.R., which indicated there was an artist in residence. One residence for an artist living and working space per building was permitted in SoHo. He was eternally grateful to Emily and to Murrimac Realty for helping him to have a secure place in the neighborhood.

"Home Sweet Home," he quietly said to himself after installing his A.I.R. sign.

As time passed, he began to spend time in his studio rather than working freelance. Qwerty felt the time had come to contact Richard, his former boss and art dealer. He looked forward to discussing his art and his career with him. The Green Gallery closed only a short time after Qwerty was drafted. Richard now worked out of a small office on Madison Avenue. He was well respected in the art world and made a living by collecting and dealing with art, writing about art and occasionally curating various projects. Qwerty located the offices and finally decided to take the subway and visit Richard. After locating the entrance to the address on Madison Avenue, he entered the office. There was a young woman at a desk. Richard appeared to be in a large office in the back.

"Richard is busy. You can wait or leave some slides of your work, and we will get back to you," she said, barely looking up from her typewriter.

Qwerty said, "Please tell Richard that Qwerty Blanc is here to see him. I'll wait."

"Qwerty Blanc, I'll be back in a minute," she said, turning and entering the back room.

"Qwerty! Where have you been?" Richard said as he came through his office door.

" I was drafted and away for a few years but returned a few years ago. I now have a studio in SoHo and am ready to show some work. Given what happened on Greene Street, do you think I will ever be able to show again?" Qwerty said, taking a seat on the office couch.

"You have got to be kidding. Your piece in the Whitney annual sculpture show in 1966 captured the attention of all the press. Clement Greenberg was hoping to see more of your work. He is putting together a major survey show for the Metropolitan Museum. I still get calls asking about you. The notoriety has turned to (legenderiety)." Richard said with a grin, proud of his new word.

"Wow, can you visit my studio and tell me what you think?"

Richard didn't hesitate. "How about a visit next week? If I see something interesting, I can call Leo about putting you in an invitational group show he is planning for next Spring."

Qwerty struggled with a large steel and flame piece in his second-floor studio workshop. He had dragged an eight-foot section of railroad track from an abandoned lot by the West Side Highway to his studio. The work of dragging the steel back to Prince Street was tedious. He hired willing passing workers from the street to get the steel up the stairs to his workshop. Once the steel was set in place in the studio, all the work was forgotten and replaced with the excitement of creating this new work. He envisioned the track becoming red hot and dangerous. Nineteenth-century technology was part of the American landscape. Most people took the rusted abandoned steel they saw along every highway and byway for granted. Qwerty saw the monstrous ego of industry. He felt it was time to strip the romantic idea of human progress and expose the environmental threat.

"I'll call this piece *Tracks of War*," he mused.

He was excited to have the track in his studio. He felt as though this track was getting an autopsy and that he was the doctor. He needed help with the technical aspect of creating a flame under the section of track. He realized he needed to develop an eight-foot-long, straight, narrow stove burner. The flame would have heat and give off carbon monoxide.

"No wonder artists paint on canvas. They don't have to worry that their painting might kill somebody," he muttered while pacing back and forth.

After days of trial and error, he asked some of the workers who did freelance metal work at Zelf Tool Rental on Greene Street for help. The equipment rental was known to every artist in SoHo.

The first thing an artist did after renting a loft was to paint the entire space white and then sand and polyurethane the wood floors. Sanding the wood floors required renting sanders from Zelf's store. In addition to floor sanders, there was a complete metal working shop that freelance metal workers used.

He entered the shop and found a friendly worker named Barry, whom Qwerty had met at Fanelli's Bar. He avoided talking to Mr. Zelf, who was tedious and anal about the use of his equipment. He described the challenges of creating his track and flame piece to Barry, and they agreed on an hourly rate for him to be hired. Barry told Qwerty that working with gas this way was tricky. He explained that there were custom gas apertures that had to be the right size for the gas distribution under the track. Barry also pointed out that the flames would require ventilation for fresh air intake and exhaust, much like a residential furnace. After making a few short pieces and making them progressively longer, they determined that eight feet in length was impossible.

A few days later, Qwerty entered the shop, and Barry was ecstatic. "We create a continuous manifold and feed the short aperture sections one at a time. It can be done at any length you need. We just need to attach a pressure regulator to find the right pressure for the length of the manifold."

Qwerty realized that the effect these linear flames created was difficult to achieve but worth the effort. Barry pointed out that they would need approval from Underwriters Laboratories to create a device that would sell. He said that if Qwerty paid the expenses, he knew someone who could start the process. He also indicated that the ventilation ductwork and fans must be part of the design. Qwerty agreed and Barry was given the task of moving forward. Qwerty knew this would take time, so he created works that used standard devices like small portable propane tank burners for camping cookware.

To prepare for Richard's studio visit, he installed two torches hidden in the corner walls at mid-ceiling height. When he turned off the studio lighting, he liked the sound and the glow in the corner. His favorite was a stream of molten solder that ran across the studio floor on a sand bed, giving the impression of molten lava. The ideas were coming faster than he could produce them.

Nomo stopped by the studio for a visit. Qwerty was delighted to see his old friend again. Nomo brought along his new video camera. He was excited to tell Qwerty about the great thing this handheld video technology was for artists.

Qwerty said "Let's try an experiment with your video."

He placed a microphone by the propane flame, turned out the lights, and pointed the video camera on the wall to catch the flickering flame.

Nomo said, "I get it!" and helped him with a few versions.

"You need to create a loop to make it play continuously. I can edit the loops in my studio."

Qwerty wasn't sure this new technology would work for exhibitions, but the video might solve the problem of dealers having to worry about setting their galleries on fire.

He set up the video projection screen and the Bunsen Burner pieces in his studio gallery for Richard's visit. The railroad track piece was in progress in his workshop. The mini volcano flow still had technical problems but was also in progress in the workshop.

He arranged for the studio visit and Richard shouted from the sidewalk on Prince Street. Qwerty tossed a sock containing the key to the front door to Richard, who was waiting below. Sometimes, opportunity knocks, and sometimes, it drops to the sidewalk.

Richard opened the door to the third floor. He was all smiles, and could sense he was in the presence of something homegrown and fresh. He was greeted by the peaceful glow of the corner flames, the sound and large scale of the video fire, and the glowing railroad track.

"Richard, what do you think about using video in a gallery environment?"

Richard paused a moment, then replied. "Slow down a minute. I am still trying to absorb all this new work. You have your own building and have created a studio full of ambitious new work. We can discuss video someday but let me catch my breath."

"I am working with my friend Nomo, who is a video artist. I think we can come up with some interesting stuff."

" Looking forward to seeing what you guys come up with, but that can wait. Qwerty Blanc, you are ready for the world. All this work blows me away. I would love to help you get on your feet exhibiting." Richard said after catching his breath.

"Far out!"

"I'll talk to Leo and a few other people who care about ideas and establishing artists. There are some good young dealers like Klaus Kertess at Bykert Gallery who can relate to artists with new ideas.

There are also some young curators at the Whitney and the Modern who are smart and sincere. Let's arrange some studio visits and you can take it from there."

"Richard, I am overwhelmed that you have taken an interest in what I am doing. I am never sure if I am doing this right."

"You are doing great work, but I must caution you that creating the work is only half the process, and getting the work out to your audience is the other half. I don't have a gallery to offer these days, but I will help you in any way I can."

After spending some time in the studio, they walked through Washington Square Park and then to One Fifth Avenue for dinner and drinks. If there ever was such a thing as the perfect Art Deco/ Jazz Age piano bar, it was One Fifth Avenue. The piano lounge and bar were popular with people following art in SoHo. The bar was lined with people intent on studying the mirror behind it for wandering eyes, and beyond the bar was a modest, well-lit dining room. The people were the main attraction here.

Richard greeted a distinguished-looking, middle-aged man seated at a table next to the vacant table reserved for them.

"Qwerty, let me introduce Gunther Reinhardt," Richard said as they approached the table.

He turned to the people seated at the table and said, "How are things in Zurich, Gunther?"

They continued with the usual pleasantries and proceeded to their table. Qwerty knew nothing of art dealer politics but sensed that there was tension between idealistic dealers like Richard and the more established types who acted behind the scenes. The dinner was elegant.

When they were leaving, Richard said, "If Gunther contacts you, watch you back. Your new work will probably get his attention. You are better off getting shows with the new generation of dealers coming on the scene. They care about their artists. This guy is playing a dark game."

Qwerty was excited about Richard's interest. As the days passed, he returned to working in the studio and enjoyed interacting with people in the neighborhood.

Alan stopped by one day, full of enthusiasm. Qwerty offered him a joint, hoping that a toke or two might take away some of his manic good cheer. Alan was prolific in creating his large white paintings, and Qwerty really liked the subtle optical effects.

"I'll be showing with Betty Parsons Gallery," Alan said, smothering an exhale in his nostrils.

Qwerty said, "Who is Betty Parsnip?"

That started a good laugh, and they passed the time enjoying Alan's good fortune. Alan thought that Betty understood his work and that they made a good team.

There was something in the ether in New York City. The art world was suddenly hip. There was a stirring in parts of the art world that artworks could be an investment. Most galleries at that time were old school and dedicated to showing works of cultural value. As sales and prices increased, most established galleries suddenly could pay their bills, and their artists enjoyed better incomes. The idea that artists could be rich still seemed far-fetched. Attending art gallery exhibits was popular and people were buying new artwork from the galleries.

It was a good time to be a young artist in SoHo.

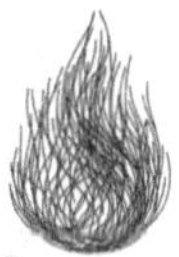

CHAPTER FOURTEEN

Getting the Show on the Road

Richard followed up his initial studio visit by recommending Qwerty's new work to curators and art dealers. One of the most important curators to visit the studio was Harald Szeeman, who was organizing *documenta 5* in Kassel, Germany. This show would feature some of the most influential art from New York and Europe. Harald selected *Tracks of War*. The sculpture took the spotlight in the revolutionary exhibition, earning rave reviews, and propelling his career to new heights."

This caught the attention of Gunther Reinhardt, the influential international art dealer and financial advisor to the rich and famous. Gunther kept a low profile, but everyone in the art world understood that he was becoming a driving force in the marketplace. He had a well-established presence in the auctions where art stolen by the Nazis during World War II was sold. Gunther's handling of these artworks and artifacts had raised concerns among established cultural institutions in Europe. Museums and auction houses grew suspicious when he started showing interest in modern art. They were wary, but the lure of money generated from his activities was irresistible.

Gunther was creating a system for the modern art market to attract investors with deep pockets. Most artists were not aware of the system being developed. Most were happy to be getting decent prices for their work. Unfortunately, the corruption of the market was spreading like a virus to corrupt the culture.

Gunther saw the modern art world as a money machine just waiting to be jump-started. His tactics were already paying off. Established Pop Artists, Abstract Expressionist Artists, and even Color-Field artists were first in line. Initially, their work was bought and auctioned at rapidly increasing prices, with little attention paid to the established value and the buyers and sellers. Quietly, a few of the prices for Abstract Expressionist stars like Willem de Kooning and Jackson Pollack began to be bought and sold routinely at extraordinarily high prices. Gunther was pitching the idea that this was only the first round. He predicted that these same works would sell for millions as time went on. This got the attention of investors in his circle. There were also established 57th Street Galleries that knew exactly where this was going. They began courting artists who had previously been associated with Leo Castelli and other galleries, which had nurtured these artists and their careers for many years..

Qwerty received a phone call one morning while he was working in the studio. A pleasant voice said, "Is this Mr. Qwerty Blanc?"

"Yes, I am," Qwerty said with some hesitation.

"Please hold for mister Gunther Reinhardt."

Gunther entered the phone conversation.

"The time for a studio visit is long overdue. I am in New York for a few days. Perhaps I could visit your studio tomorrow morning."

"I am honored, Gunther, but I am booked solid."

"Qwerty, you have no idea how much better you could be doing. There is a world out there that I can introduce you to."

"I appreciate your interest," Gunther.

"I'll stop by your studio on Prince Street tomorrow at ten o'clock if that works for you."

The next day at precisely ten o'clock, Qwerty threw the sock and key down to the Prince Street sidewalk for the limo driver. He remembered Richard's warning when he introduced Gunther. There was no harm in hearing what he had to say if he indeed watched his back in the process.

Qwerty improved the safety and reliability of the works. He developed a similar relationship to the work that parents have with their children. His custody of these new creations required making sure that they behaved. He felt confident that they were ready for the world. Gunther was part of this new world.

Qwerty showed Gunther the works in progress on the studio floors. Gunther's reaction surprised Qwerty.

"This work is fantastic. I think we can take your career to the top." Gunther said as they sat on the roof garden drinking wine. "You just make art and I'll take care of the rest. How does that sound? I'll draw up a contract, and we can make some money."

"I only take cash, and I avoid interviews and personal photos," Qwerty replied.

"No problem, Qwerty. I like cash and can handle all the paperwork," Gunther said while dumping some white powder from a small amber bottle on the coffee table.

Gunther chopped up a series of lines. "Do you like cocaine? "

"I like smoking pot with my friends, but I haven't quite got the hang of cocaine."

Gunther rolled up a hundred-dollar bill, snorted two lines, and offered it to Qwerty after drinking more wine and snorting more cocaine. Qwerty finally replied to Gunther's statement about a contract.

"It's your money, Gunther, so I don't want to sign a contract. Let's just shake on it. Okay?"

Qwerty then took Gunther downstairs to show him his secret project.

In a small room in the studio on the fourth floor, Qwerty had taken a globe of the earth and suspended it from the ceiling. In the center of the globe, he had installed red light bulbs. He had drilled holes at the North and South Pole to allow the red light to shine through. When he turned down the lights in the studio, the globe emitted two beams of red light from the globe at each pole.

Qwerty explained, "This is a model of the earth. The project that I dream of is to create two separate light beams into space during the Equinox. They would be photographed from satellites. It would be as if the earth were sending streams of fire from the core. I don't think we could get the technology for the lights right now, but anything is possible at some point in the future."

"Big idea, Qwerty. No one can accuse you of not thinking big. Maybe we could get some foundation to fund this one day. I can't imagine how this could be marketed, so we will just let this one sit for a while."

After Gunther left, Qwerty was feeling anxious, withdrawing from the cocaine. He decided that he didn't understand why cocaine was such a big deal. It wasn't worth the withdrawal and the amount of alcohol it took to mellow out. The idea of Gunther handling his career made him even more anxious. There is a process that only an experienced artist understands. The process starts with an idea that springs forward from somewhere deep in the subconscious. The idea then has a life of its own. It persists and demands attention. Finally, the battle to act on the concept happens in the studio. There are no outside forces. No dealers, no critics, and no economics are welcomed. It is personal and private and sometimes lonely. Often there is a moment of euphoria. What follows is beyond the control of the artist. When the process has run its course, the art leaves the sanctuary of the studio and takes on a life of its own.

Qwerty felt that he could rely on the opinions of dealers like Richard, who saw their work as an integral part of the art. Gunther was someone who shed no light on the process of making art and had no concern for the artist or the artwork.

Qwerty was glad to be alone in his studio. He looked at his fiddle case hanging on the wall and decided it was a good time to visit the

Village. Greenwich Village was always a playground of distractions, offering the perfect escape for him to discover new and invigorating experiences.

Chapter Fifteen

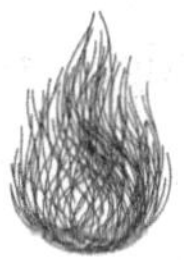

Nomo and His Ride

Nomo awoke from a dream in his loft on the Bowery. In his dream, an alpha male wolf's eyes reflected gold in the light of the springtime Arctic sun. There was the sound of crackling ice from his paws breaking through the snow as he approached the ridge of the mountain range overlooking a valley with a river and herds of caribou grazing on the exposed grass in the valley below. He looked back at his newly formed pack and felt the weight of responsibility he had assumed. The wolf ruled the magnificent valley and claimed this territory to raise and protect his pack.

He lay in his bed for a while, savoring his vision of the wolf. He wondered why he would dream of power and territory. "I have no time to dwell on this; I need to find a new project to film," he said to himself while he dressed.

Nomo's loft was in a four-story building just south of Cooper Union above a store called Bowery Electric. It was time to pay the rent to Lester, the owner of Bowery Electric and his landlord. As he entered the store, he noticed that Bowery Electric had purchased a new van. The old green Ford with the Bowery Electric signage and a bit of graffiti had a for-sale sign and was parked behind the new truck. Nomo greeted Lester with a smile.

"Morning Lester, it's that time of the month. What's with the new van?"

Lester was much like his building and business: old, crusty, and straightforward. "You want to buy the old van?"

Nomo thought for a second and replied, "Sure, 200 bucks?" Lester didn't hesitate. He filled out a bill of sale and signed the title over without any conversation.

Papers in hand, Nomo boarded the subway to register the van. The Motor Vehicle office on Chambers Street was always an adventure. The large open lobby was packed with lines of impatient people. Today, Nomo saw lines stretching from the doors to the tellers. He filled out his papers and wondered if he wanted to deal with the wait.

Artists usually have no patience for bureaucracy, but Nomo was looking forward to being able to drive his van about town. He waited his turn and had his registration in hand.

After finishing up at the Motor Vehicles office, Nomo walked to Bayard Street for lunch at his favorite Thai restaurant. A middle-aged man who owned the restaurant greeted him at the door. When he saw Nomo, he assumed a King Fu pose.

"Bruce Lee!" the owner exclaimed.

"OK, I'm back," Nomo replied with his own Kung Fu pose.

Nemo didn't have the heart to disappoint him by telling him he was not Bruce Lee. In New York City, there are times when a doppelgänger can be mistaken for a movie star. Tribeca was nearby, attracting actors, directors, and producers from Hollywood. It was not uncommon to see famous people in the neighborhoods.

After lunch, Nomo screwed the plates on his van and drove to Prince Street to see Qwerty.

He parked at the corner of Greene Street and yelled for Qwerty to come down.

Qwerty walked up to the truck laughing. "You didn't buy that piece of crap, did you?"

Nomo rubbed the top a bit. "Yup, she's all mine."

Laughing, they climbed aboard, lit a joint, and took a reckless spin up and down West Broadway. As they drove Nomo described his dream about the wolf taking ownership of the magnificent arctic valley.

"Wow, you must be feeling powerless about your career," Qwerty said without hesitation.

"That sucks; maybe I just like wildlife," Nomo fired back.

Qwerty realized that his comment had stung his friend a bit, so he added, "Hey man, we are wildlife, and the art world is our habitat. Every artist wants to believe that their work is on a ground that is not inhabited by anyone else. Let's face it, we are territorial. This art is mine, and if you rip me off, I will tear your heart out."

Nomo looked at Qwerty and said, "You own fire. Nobody dares to imitate what you do. But I am feeling lost. Everybody thinks they are video artists, and the differences in their work are difficult to identify. I need a big idea, a big statement, and I need to tell my own story."

"Poor baby," Qwerty said, stroking his finger on his cheek.

"Up yours, Q-man."

When they returned to the 106 Prince Street studio, Qwerty said, "Hey, I have this idea that we could work on together. The idea is to create a room that looks like the walls are in flames and filled with the sound of chaotic fire."

Nomo yelled out, "Go to Hell!"

He quietly added, "That would be the title."

Qwerty shook his head, "Jerk."

"Hey, let's head over to Fanelli's and get wasted. We'll celebrate your new wheels and our going to Hell," Qwerty added.

They had formed a bond that happens to people who are walking a lonely path together. This night was an opportunity to do whiskey shots with draft beer chasers and enjoy each other's company.

"So, Q-man, you never talk about your past and where you come from," Nomo said. " What happens in New York stays in New York, eh buddy?"

Qwerty replied, "Nomo, you are the only person I can trust with my secrets. It is just not time to discuss all that."

They returned to Qwerty's studio to get started on "Go to Hell." They became two children turned loose in a playground.

Chapter Sixteen

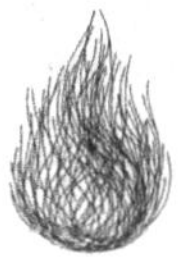

Omfug Now What

Nomo's Bowery studio was a few blocks north of a club called CBGBs. During the day, the club blended in with its Bowery neighbors, which also contained businesses with no-nonsense names like Flats Fixed. At night, the scene outside the club transformed into a noisy mass of fans with bizarre hairdos and pierced noses. The outside chaos was serene compared with the volume and rhythm of the music inside.

Like most nightclubs, dancers moved to the rhythm and beat of the music. At CBGBs, the bodies were in awkward motion and the music had the appearance of a cry for help during a fire. There were a few rules for the bands, but there seemed to be no rules for customers. The liquor was watered down and expensive. Most customers didn't care because they brought their own drugs. The drug of choice was a combination of speed and mixed psychedelics.

The typical patron was known as a punk, a term borrowed from the London music scene. The label didn't fit Nomo exactly, but he related to the message. He regularly spent nights at the club with his portable video camera, filming and getting to know some of the musicians. Some musicians that were invited by the management showed great promise and creativity. Some groups were somewhere south of awful. He loved the music scene and found himself torn between the art videos created for the galleries and his music videos. He wondered where his music videos would be shown. They were created on a hunch that they would develop a new audience.

Nomo hoped that Gunther might find a market for his video works. He struggled to pay his bills and asked Qwerty if he could arrange a studio visit. Qwerty made the arrangements, and Gunther reluctantly arrived at Nomo's Bowery studio building.

Gunther's limo arrived at the Bowery Electric building and told his driver to wait. Qwerty never appreciated how Gunther talked to his staff or working people. To be clear, he considered Gunther a condescending asshole but decided from the start that Gunther was part of his life and career whether he liked it or not. They entered the building and proceeded up the dark and dirty stairwell.

"I know that Nomo is your best friend, but I am not going to promote his work," Gunther said, stopping at the first landing.

"What are you saying, Gunther? Nomo is one of the best video artists around. The work he did with me was amazing. I think you are making a big mistake."

"Do me a favor, Qwerty. Stay out of my business. It is over your head. Just do your thing and leave the business to me."

They continued in silence to Nomo's studio. As he opened the door, Nomo grinned from ear to ear like a Cheshire Cat. He had set up his video projection of the "Go to Hell" piece for Qwerty and Gunther. Nomo spun around in a dervish dance as the piece went into action.

"That's fantastic," Qwerty said with a grin that matched Nomo's perfectly.

"What is this?" Gunther asked.

"This is a new piece that Nomo and I are collaborating on called "Go to Hell." This piece is designed for an isolated gallery room. The entry has two torches on each side. A motion detector enables a video of huge flames projected on each wall as people walk into the room. They are engulfed in the images of fire."

"So…they have gone to Hell!" Nomo exclaimed with more grins and chuckles.

"Fantastic boys, but who is going to buy that? Okay, maybe a museum exhibit or some such." Gunther paused, turned to Qwerty, and said," Actually, I know someone who might love it. I'll make a call."

Gunther turned to Nomo and said, "I think you are doing wonderful work, but I have decided to go with a Korean video artist who has caught the attention of the critics and the market by using monitors and projections. I can't support two different artists at the same time. It's just not good for business."

Nomo was stunned. This news meant that he had lost the turf war, kicked off the merry-go-round, taken off the field and benched.

"Okay, I think I would like to be alone," Nomo said, walking to the window and silently staring down at the sidewalk.

Qwerty and Gunther quietly let themselves out the door to the stairway. Qwerty stopped at a landing and said to Gunther, "Am I the next one to be dumped?"

Gunther replied, "Oh no. You are a potential gold mine. We are in the process of selling your career to the DIA Foundation. They will, of course, prepare a written contract that will provide you with a monthly stipend, arrange future exhibits, place your work in museum collections, and create permanent exhibition spaces in various locations. They will provide you with assistance, materials, and cover expenses. They will also determine if any new work is appropriate.

Qwerty was utterly dumbfounded. He had never heard of such an arrangement, and the idea of packaging his career and having some organization take over was shocking. "What exactly do you mean by new work?"

Gunther laughed and said, "You really haven't been paying attention to the art world. DIA has made similar arrangements with several major modern artists. It is a win-win situation for art that isn't easily marketed, like standard painting and sculpture. They have the resources to exhibit and distribute the work. Win, win, win. Relax, Qwerty. You will be among the immortals, buddy. We'll talk some more. Bye-bye now."

Qwerty walked back up the stairs, shaking his head. He heard loud drumming from the apartment on the floor below Nomo. The drumming was followed by the electric guitars that sounded more like chainsaws than musical instruments. Qwerty continued up to console Nomo.

When he approached Nomo, he said, "That sucks, man. I'm sorry, but we talked about how the art world is driven by territory."

Nomo just looked him in the eye and said, "Fuck him anyway. I met some TV people who are working on something new that seems to be catching on big time."

"Okay, I am all ears, Nomo."

Nomo offered some tea, and they sat at the table. Nomo took a breath and said, "Okay, do you hear that music downstairs? That group is called the Dumbfugs, and they are a hot thing at the CBGB club down the street. They just learned to play their instruments, but they are wildly popular. It doesn't matter how musical they are; it is all about energy. I loved making videos of them playing. The videos pick up on that energy and I edit in other images to suit the song. We are creating a kind of music video combination from live performances. We put it on tape right now, but there are TV people talking about putting them on cable channel TV. I think they might even pay me good money. So, to hell with Gunther and his art hype."

Qwerty was relieved, "Let's hit the streets and forget about fucking Gunther."

There's something about the times in which artists live that can take them to unexpected places. Nomo didn't realize that his videos would bring the musicians' vision to millions through the emerging medium of MTV. This opportunity took him beyond the art world to places he had never imagined.

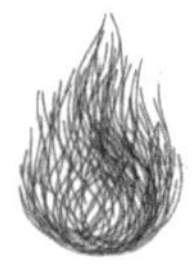

Chapter Seventeen

Up Yonder

The energy of street life in SoHo depended on the weather. On this rainy spring day, Qwerty gazed out his window at the street below. There were puddles, litter, and a few scattered people with umbrellas shielding their identities and purposes. As he gazed, his mind wandered. The sound of his phone brought him back from his musing.

"Is this Hank Smith?" the voice asked.

"Yes indeed."

"This is Mary McClellan Hospital calling for your mother, Alice."

"Is everything alright?"

"We think you should come to the hospital as soon as possible to be with your mother. She is quite ill."

Qwerty was numb and answered, "I will be there as soon as possible."

He quickly threw together some clothes and snacks, grabbed some cash and called Nomo to borrow his van. The weather driving up the Thruway and the local roads suited his mood. The sky was grey, with even grayer clouds passing low overhead. The wipers were old, which made focusing on the road tedious. He pushed the limits of the van and the speed limit on the Thruway, arriving at the hospital early in the evening.

He had stopped at the grocery store and purchased a small bouquet. Looking at the flowers as he opened the door to Alice's room, he took a breath and decided to be at least as cheerful as the flowers appeared. Alice lay propped up in bed with oxygen tubes across her face.

"Hey," he said, smiling and extending his hand.

"Hey," Alice replied as tears ran down her cheeks.

"What's up, Mom?"

Alice looked away and said, "I'm nervous and a little scared because I don't know what is next."

Qwerty realized she was dying. New York City and his life there faded away as he returned to his childhood and the warmth and love that Alice provided. The child in him didn't want to face losing her, but the man he had become knew that it was his turn to provide love and comfort to her.

Alice turned her face to Qwerty and said, "You may not know this, but I have been following your secret life in New York City. I went to the library and looked at the art magazines and the art section in the Sunday Times. I am so proud of you. I realized that you chose to keep it secret around here, and I kept it to myself. I never even told Adam. You have been blessed with a gift God gave you to pass on to the world. Always be true to a gift from the Lord."

Qwerty felt tears running down his cheeks and squeezed her hand. "You'll get better, and I can take you home soon. Right?"

"No, Hank. The old ticker is just worn out and I am going to pass. I need you to tell me that you love me and that I shouldn't worry about what comes next because I'll be in the Good Shepherd's hands."

Qwerty had always struggled with all the things that Sunday school and the church had offered as undeniable truth. Alice often said that you take what you need and leave the rest at the door. From an early age, young Hank preferred to leave everything at the door. For Alice's sake, Qwerty decided to go back in and hope for the best.

"You know son, when I look out that window, I can see my mom and dad waving on the other side of yonder river. I do believe they are just waiting for me to cross." A moment later, he felt her hand relax. Her journey had begun.

Hank did his best to gather his emotions and return to Adam at the farm. He found Adam in his recliner in the living room.

"Our wonderful lady is gone, Adam," Hank said, reaching down to hug Adam.

"I am glad you are here. Together, we can give Alice a proper send-off."

Hank and Adam made the arrangements for Alice's funeral with the help of the local funeral home. Announcements and obituaries appeared in the local paper, and the small community prepared to say goodbye to one of its most popular citizens.

It was a beautiful day for Alice's funeral. The air was crisp and fresh, and the sunshine was warm and comforting. Qwerty took a break from thoughts of his life in New York City to become Hank Smith again and savor the benefits of growing up in a small, tight-knit community. It appeared that everyone in the township had come to say goodbye to Alice. Everyone in town knew Alice as the dedicated Town Clerk who was actively involved in church and community service.

He relished the opportunity just to be good old Hank Smith again. It was surprisingly easy to do. Everyone was focused on the sadness of the loss of Alice. Adam had arranged a gathering at the farm for folks to meet and share stories. Most people gathered at the farm didn't drink alcohol, but Adam had set up a bar with unblended Irish whiskey for those who did. Adam poured Hank a glass, clicked the glasses, and saluted Alice. Hank had never seen Adam drink alcohol. The Irish whiskey was a pleasant source of bonding.

"The farm is in your name now, Hank. That was Alice's last request. You know that we both love you, and we know you will take good care of this beautiful land."

Hank realized how much Adam and Alice meant to him at that moment. "I don't think I ever told you I love you, Adam. You and Alice have always been good to me. I have always considered the two of you as Mom and Dad."

The sun was setting, and people were still arriving. A young woman stepped out of a red Jeep. The top was down, and the sides were open, giving it a sporting look. She walked up to him and introduced herself. She was fit, tall and proud.

"My name is Lauretta with the letters au, but everyone spells it with the letter o because that's how Loretta Lynn spells the name. Just call me Rett."

"The last time I saw you was way back in high school. I didn't think you were very friendly but maybe you didn't smile much because of the braces."

"I didn't think you were very friendly because you were a jerk," Rett said with a grin.

"We are all sad about losing Alice. She was a very special lady and always showed concern and support to others. I spent a lot of time here hiking and fishing on the river at her farm." she added.

"What are you up to these days?" Hank asked.

"I am working on my master's degree thesis in environmental studies. I want to come back here and do my part to save what is left of this beautiful countryside. It is special and worth protecting."

"I am impressed. I think you have an important goal." Hank said.

"What do you do in New York City?' she asked.

"It's complicated. I create artwork and have found a passion that is hard to explain. For that matter, I haven't really figured it out for myself. When I do, I will let you know." In saying that, Hank realized that if he wanted to get to know her better, that explanation fell short of the mark. There was something about Rett he hadn't found in the women he had dated in the city.

Her eyes were clear, and she seemed to be surrounded by a soothing natural aura.

"I've got some flyrods here in the house. Would you like to head down to the river for an evening of fishing?" Hank asked.

"I would love that," she replied. "I was hoping we could spend some time togehter before you head back to your mysterious life in the city."

The evening sun was filtering down through the leaves of the maples and sycamores along the Battenkill as they crossed the bridge at Center Falls and along the fields on their way down to the river. Rett changed into shorts and rubber shoes, and Hank wore a bathing suit. The air along the river valley was noticeably cooler and there was an amber haze above the river. Tiny bubbles formed and disappeared along the riffles created by rocks interrupting the water's flow. Lime green mayflies rose from the river surface, ready for their moment of love and creation of the next generation. For the trout, it was a moment to enjoy a summer feast. Rett and Hank were knee-deep in the flowing water, casting their flies and lost in the moment. They were in the flow and united in their connection to the river. They managed to catch a few trout, which they released unharmed back into their mysterious hiding places beneath the ripples of water. The couple seemed grateful simply to make the connection to the river. They sat on the bank as the sun set, taking it all in. Hank ran back to the farmhouse and returned with a basket containing some red wine, a baguette, and brie.

"Heart be still. You are a city slicker, aren't you, Hank?" Rett smiled.

"I thought Reverend Ryman did a nice job on the service for Alice," Hank said as they sat by the riverbank, enjoying their company and the treats.

Rett laughed as she recalled Reverend Ryman's words. "Yes, the train pulled into the station and took our beloved Alice away. But don't you worry that train is BOUND for Glory. Amen."

"Amen," Hank added and moved closer for a kiss. "I am going to be away for a while but perhaps I could call you when I return."

"I would like that," Rett added, returning his kiss.

Hank wrote down her local telephone number and drew a heart around it. She said she would finish her studies at Cornell and stay in touch. They gave each other a polite kiss but would have liked to go much further.

An unusual warm feeling entered Hank as he waved to Rett's Jeep as she drove away.

That year, Hank returned once again for Adam's funeral. He found a neighbor who agreed to maintain the farm. He also called Rett from time to time to make sure he didn't lose touch. Driving back to the city each time, he imagined himself married to her and having children. Rett made it very clear that she could never live in any city, so a big decision had to be made about his life.

Qwerty was created in the city and may have to die there too. He had loved his early studio days totally and without reservation, but his city world was changing. The artists in SoHo were either getting rich, with houses in East Hampton or remaining poor and mysteriously disappearing. Qwerty missed those Saturday chatter fests at the local bars after a day of looking at the latest offerings in the galleries. He also began to feel the annoying pressure Gunther was putting on him, affecting his focus and love of being in the studio. The art that had transformed his spirit was suddenly being compromised by the very success that it had created.

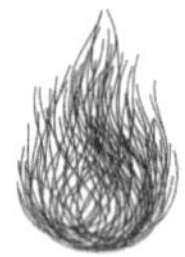

CHAPTER EIGHTEEN

Au Canada

Patrons of the arts generally have managed to make a lot of money. If you divided them into two groups, there would be one group obsessed with making money and one blessed with good fortune. They both enjoy spending money in July and August. There is no point in having millions in the bank if you can't sail along the Amalfi Coast and dine on local rabbit dishes in a hilltop restaurant in Ischia. Perhaps renting a stone cottage in Arles, France, to contemplate Van Gogh would refresh the spirit. The options for places to enjoy in summer is only limited to the imagination. Spending the summer in Manhattan with the back of the neck getting sweaty and gritty is not an option.

Summer for the art world was a time to give the artist's studios and the dealer's galleries a rest. The focus of exhibitions shifted to other cities and countries. These alternate venues welcomed New York artists. The local venues benefit from the prestige of the works on loan. There is something refreshing about the mix of local personalities and people in their communities in the festive atmosphere of summer. People mix art with good food, families, and the summer sun. Sharing this experience is one of the perks of being a well-known New York artist.

Toronto was home to a rising economic force, along with a growing interest in art. The art community was closely tied to the young dealers and artists exhibiting in SoHo. Qwerty received an invitation to participate in an invitational group show at the David Mirvish Gallery in Toronto. The exhibition was formed to feature New York-based paintings and sculptures in a newly expanded gallery space on Markham Street.

He rented a car and drove via the Northway. After an overnight campground stop at the Thousand Islands, he approached Toronto. He was disappointed it didn't have a skyline like New York City. There is something comforting about a city skyline that draws visitors to the center. New York's skyline was a benchmark for knowing where you are in relation to the center.

He brought a road map that didn't detail the streets of Toronto. Fortunately, he exited the highway into downtown Toronto at a sign for the University of Toronto. His hunch was that a university might be near art galleries. The hunch paid off. He saw a middle-aged man with shorts and a baseball hat with an unusually long visor. With his skinny legs and round belly, you might describe him as a birdman. Qwerty rolled down his window to ask the birdman directions.

"Excuse me, sir, how can I get to Markham Street and the Mirvish Gallery?"

He stopped, turned to the car, and said, "Oh, Jeez, Markham Street. If it was a snake, it would jump right up and bite ya! Just make your first left up ahead and it runs right into Markham. The gallery isn't far from Honest Eds."

"Honest Ed's, great. Thank You." In New York City, there are stores with names like Crazy Eddie's. In Toronto, there are stores with names like Honest Ed's. "Go figure," Qwerty mused.

He located the gallery on Markham Street with the birdman's directions. It was impressive in scale and well-designed. The reception area was much like that of a New York gallery. On the table was a summary of the show. It featured Qwerty with a resume that he hadn't seen before. Seeing their version of his history in black and white was interesting.

"May I help you?" the receptionist asked.

"Hi, my name is Qwerty Blanc. I just drove up from New York."

"Amanda. Wow, Qwerty Blanc. I love your work."

"In that case, will you marry me?"

"You could at least offer a dinner and drinks first."

"I am up for that. Let's have dinner."

"David said you might be coming today for the opening tonight. There is a room for you at his friend's compound on the lake. I'll take you there. We could have that dinner you offered on the way."

The lakeshore was lovely, with lots of boats and activity. The compound jutted out from the harbor on a rocky ledge. There was a large open room that opened out to a deck. Apparently, the owner had inherited an extensive collection of taxidermy. There were all sorts of horned animal heads on the wall, zebra and bear skin rugs on the floor, and the most disturbing was an elephant foot poof. Along the way, Qwerty and the receptionist exchanged pleasantries and were attracted to each other. Amanda showed Qwerty a series of joined bungalows that had separate bathrooms. When they got to his room, there was a small bar setup, and the summer sun was setting in the evening sky. Qwerty was feeling giddy and decided to be completely inappropriate.

"Hey, let's get drunk and fuck." he said with a laugh. To his surprise, Amanda poured two drinks and unbuttoned her blouse. So, they did.

Qwerty had created an updated version of his original "Fire and Rain" piece for the occasion. He saw the piece set up in a separate small room. He was always impressed at the ability of art gallery workers to set up works for exhibiting artists. The installation was perfect.

The gallery reception was well attended despite the off-season when most collectors would be out of town. The public and press well attended the opening, and the mood was quite pleasant and festive. As usual, Qwerty made a point of staying out of the limelight. He kept looking at Amanda doing her gallery socializing and enjoyed thinking about his good fortune that evening. He knew that it was a one-shot deal and not to make more of it. Despite the mild disappointment, she was a pleasure to look at.

"Qwerty!" Standing behind him was Michael, an artworld lawyer who handled legal affairs for Gunther.

"Michael, I am glad you are here. I need to hire you and it's important. I need you to create a last will and set up the Qwerty Blanc Foundation for me. I am naming my friend Nomo as the sole trustee. The building on Prince Street will remain in trust for the foundation. I'll drop off the information and sign everything at your office when I return to New York."

"Wow. That is a lot of work, but sure, I can do that. See you at the after party." Michael said with a sly smile.

"Great," Qwerty replied. He would have rather said something like, "Not if I see you first."

Later that evening, the artists and gallery owner had an after-party at the compound. Amanda wasn't there. Qwerty recognized some of the artists at the party. Most were painters except for a sculptor who worked in industrial steel. He exchanged pleasantries, drank, and enjoyed some time on the deck overlooking the lake.

When he entered a small hall that contained the African hunting trophies, Michael had laid out some coke on a glass table. The coke party habit was catching on with the rich and the not-so-rich. They all seemed to have the same devices. Michael, of course, had a little mirror with his business card printed on the back and a gold-plated razor blade. Naturally, a hundred-dollar bill was rolled up to snort. Qwerty never quite got the rich people's fascination with coke. The only thing he noticed was that he talked too much and felt like he was falling in love with every pretty girl he talked to.

As the party thinned out, Qwerty felt like going to his room for the night. Michael cozied up to him on the couch, put his arm around him, and handed him a pill.

"Take this. It will help you come down from the coke. Wash it down with this," he said, handing him some scotch.

Qwerty began to feel light-headed, and Michael ran his hands on Qwerty's body.

In his mind, he was thinking what a creep Michael was with his date rape pills and coke. He managed to get to his feet and head toward his room. He needed to keep a hand on the wall to keep from falling.

He looked back at Michael and said, "Just get that legal work set up, asshole."

When he returned to his room, he crashed into his bed and fell into a deep sleep.

The next morning, he was hung over and questioned his relationship with Gunther and the characters like Michael, who served the rich and famous. The rewards of dealing with these characters didn't seem worth the cost to his integrity. He needed a break.

The summer sun cut through the sheer white curtains in the bungalow window, making Qwerty's eyes water. His mouth was parched, and he walked to the lodge where breakfast was waiting. The artists and their friends greeted him with good cheer. He thanked everyone for the hospitality, packed the trunk of the car, and drove away.

As he drove to downtown Toronto, the local newspaper article Alice discussed with him about his high school friend Bernie came to mind. The article featured Bernie sitting at a desk in an office in Toronto for American boys who needed help in relocating from the

US to Canada to avoid the draft. Qwerty thought that seeing Bernie would be a breath of fresh air.

The office was the Toronto Anti Draft Programme headquarters on Yonge Street. He located the address, but the office was no longer in use. The war and the draft were no longer the hotbed issues that they had been in the late nineteen sixties. In the hallway, he met a young woman who dressed the part of an anti-war period hipster.

Qwerty asked, "Excuse me, miss. I am looking for my friend Bernie, who used to work at the Toronto Anti Draft Programme on this floor."

"Jeez, Bernie. That was a long time ago. Bernie, Jeez. Oh ya, he is a well-known guitar and fiddle player. Try looking him up at the Toronto Musician's Union."

"I'll do that. Thanks." He said as he headed back to the street and a phone booth.

The Toronto Musician's Union had Bernie's information. They gave Qwerty the address and even directions to Bernie's apartment. He was a bit nervous to see Bernie by surprise after all these years. He parked his car and knocked on the apartment door. The last time that Qwerty had seen Bernie, he was a seventeen-year-old with a freckled face. When the door opened, Qwerty saw a burly fellow with a large black beard and sparkling eyes.

"Bernie?"

"Hank?"

"It has been a long time and a long road since I saw you last," Qwerty said, tears forming in his eyes.

"I don't get to see many old friends from home. There is an amnesty now, but my life is here. I am officially a Canuck now." Bernie said while reaching out for a hug.

"Do you like being a Canadian?"

"Man, that's a complicated question. I have helped others to become citizens of Canada. I even helped write the manual that people use to emigrate. I am so involved in my music now that I have put being an American in the past. Come on in; you can stay upstairs tonight, and we can catch up on old times."

After unloading his car, Bernie gave him a tour of his apartment and sleeping quarters. Bernie suggested a Chinese dinner. The restaurant was classic Chinese. It reminded Qwerty of the second-story restaurants on a winding street just off Chatham Square in New York. One from column "A" and two from Column "B." Perfect for Gringos with no knowledge of Chinese cuisine. Bernie knew just what to order since he was a regular customer. The waiters were not as nasty as they were in New York. They were quite pleasant and offered a refreshing Canadian hospitality. Soon, they were enjoying a tasty meal.

"So, what happened when you arrived in Toronto, Bernie? I read an article in the local paper Alice sent me in which they had your picture at an office for American draft dodgers to help them get settled in Canada. How did that happen?"

"Hank, it was a trip. My sister Naomi was involved in the Students for a Democratic Society in college. They had formed an organization called the Student Union for Peace Action, helping people emigrate to Canada to avoid the draft. When I came to Toronto, they had formed an office called the Toronto Anti-Draft Programme. I located the offices. It wasn't very impressive or organized. There were people answering the phone and sitting at second-hand desks. Someone was crashing on a sofa. I said that I would like to help with what they were doing. One counselor stopped what he was doing, stood up, and said, "Here are the keys." I remember being dumbfounded. I helped run the place for a few years until someone else walked in, asked to help, and I handed him the keys."

They laughed as one. Qwerty was delighted to find out what an interesting and funny man Bernie had become. In high school, Bernie was his catcher when he pitched for the baseball team. They were just two kids trying to figure out what everyone else seemed to know. At this moment, they were men who knew what others knew and perhaps a bit more.

"I was drafted into the Army, Bernie. I didn't spend much time in Nam because I got busted up getting out of a Chinook. Never even got a chance to shoot back. Didn't want to be there anyway."

"That was your choice, Hank. I choose not to let them put me there."

"Ouch! I suppose I deserve that. Bernie, we never talked much as kids about anything important, so if you don't mind me asking, how did you make that choice?"

Bernie went back to his lunch for a bit and finally said, "I didn't really have to think about it very much. I was never an intellectual or had much concern about politics. My father had the chicken farm, and my mom was a teacher. We did have some communist relatives, but I didn't pay much attention to them. I didn't think allowing myself to be drafted was an option for me. The War in Vietnam was wrong, evil, and a big lie. America was the Cold War superpower that supposedly never did anything wrong. You know, the good guys, the cowboys with the white hats. The war forced me to be political."

"I get it Bernie, you acted on your principles. You didn't give in to a society that said you owe them something for being born in Upstate New York. You looked them in the eye and said I don't need your fucking approval."

"Hank, you were the all-American boy back then. Alice and Adam took you to church on Sunday and you were a popular student in school. Our family was Jewish, so we weren't part of your church community. I was an average student and not doctor or lawyer material. Now I am a Canadian guitar and fiddle player happy as a clam."

"You know Bernie, that when I got drafted, I didn't want to go. I hated the War in Vietnam but didn't give a shit about it until the government reached out and bit me on the ass. Then I cared. I was too morally lazy and self-centered to do what you did. It was the path of least resistance to do what was expected of me. It haunts me to this day that I was a people pleaser and might offend someone. I couldn't imagine shaming Alice and Adam and our little town by dodging the draft."

"I am glad you see it that way, Hank. A lot of people back home consider me a traitor."

"You're not the traitor, Bernie. I am. I let myself get involved in things that I know are wrong because I cared more about my reputation than my soul."

Bernie and Hank had just exchanged more over lunch conversation than in all the years they spent together growing up. It was time to return to New York. Bernie had made difficult choices. His decision to serve his conscience severed his relationship with the community. The decision also set him on a course with new experiences and communities that held great promise. His new country welcomed him.

Qwerty wasn't sure he would ever see Bernie again, but he was sure that Bernie would have a rich and full life. Life had blown Qwerty around like a feather in the wind. He had accepted everything at face value. Perhaps it was time to follow Bernie's example and use the feathers as wings.

Chapter Nineteen

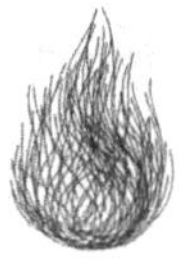

Sacred Objects

It was September, and it was an exciting time in SoHo in the second half of the 1970s. The art world was full of energy, and expectations were high for a new season of shows with fresh works and ideas. Qwerty was preparing for another New York show, and the works were, for the most part, complete. He experienced that brief period when an artist believed his works were quite good. Panic would come later as the shows were being installed. For now, it was time just to savor the process.

Solitude is often an artist's best friend. It visits at times that are not expected or planned. Without announcing itself, it occupies the mind and replaces all the plans, ambitions, and even desires for some sort of pleasure or satisfaction. The mind becomes a blank canvas, and time stops to allow the muse to visit and the spirit within to rest and replenish itself. There were times to sit in a comfortable chair in the studio, light a beeswax candle, and stare at the flame.

Sitting before his beeswax candle, he remembered all the good times in his boyhood with Adam and Alice on the farm tending to the beehives. Adam had about ten hives he would nurture and sell honey at the farmer's market. Qwerty loved searching for the queen bee through the hives and assessing the brood. Adam would explain all the finer points of the hive's life throughout the seasons. There was always a challenge and something new to learn from Adam and the bees themselves. The hive would draw him into their consciousness. Like the individual bees, he needed to join the collective brain to find a fresh perspective.

Every time Qwerty lit one of the beeswax candles, he felt the presence of a collective spirit greater than himself. Adam had passed away that summer, and Qwerty felt the loss. Adam created a moral compass that kept him on course throughout his life. Adam's passing reminded Qwerty that his own moral compass needed to be calibrated.

As he looked around the studio, he noticed a collection of what looked like bones on his table.

He couldn't remember exactly who gave them to him or why, but he was told they were from one of the many great mounds located in the Mississippi Valley built by the indigenous people before the Europeans arrived. He stared at the candle and fondled the objects.

The phone rang and broke the spell.

"Qwerty, this is Crow Dog. We are coming to New York City."

Qwerty felt a rush of mixed feelings. He had spent time with Leonard Crow Dog purely by chance. He traveled to New Mexico with an artist friend who was moving to Santa Fe. She relocated to paint the desert and emulate Georgia O'Keeffe, who lived nearby. When they arrived in New Mexico, they stayed at a wonderful adobe house on the Rio Grande, which the artist's friend had built and lived in. He had also built an authentic teepee that had served as his first residence while he completed his house.

He had good relations with the Native American community. The American Indian Movement was active there, and Leonard Crow Dog, a Sioux medicine man from the Rosebud Reservation, was invited to join in some ceremonies. One of the ceremonies was held at the artist's friend's teepee. Qwerty attended an all-night ceremony and morning sweat lodge with Leonard and a group of his relatives and friends.

Afterward, Qwerty used his van to deliver the group to the Rosebud on his way back to New York. He was fascinated by the West. The landscape, food and people were a new experience for him. He loved being part of the Native American group traveling with him. They were mostly young people that Leonard was guiding back to the traditional ways. Their experiences in urban life away from the reservation had set their values adrift. Qwerty's values were adrift in similar ways. He could relate to their predicament. Leonard's friend Stewart, a minister, created a card for Qwerty to carry in his wallet that indicated that Qwerty Blanc was a member of the Native American Church. The police might discover peyote if they were pulled over. As a member of the Native American Church, he could claim the peyote in the van was for religious purposes. All these memories rushed into Qwerty's head as he heard Leonard's voice.

"I am happy to hear from you. Would you like to stay with me? I have lots of room."

Crow Dog got right to the point: "Thank you. I am coming with Mary and the kids and picking up some young brothers that I will be taking back to the Rosebud."

" I have a building at 106 Prince Street, the same address I gave you when I stayed over at Crow Dog's Paradise. Man, it is great to know you're coming. I thought about you last summer. I was thinking about going to the Sundance you have there."

"Maybe you just weren't ready."

"When are you coming?"

"We are in Ohio, so probably tomorrow."

"See you then, just call from the street, and I will let you in."

Qwerty sat back in his chair and let the surprise of a visit from Crow Dog sink in. He was a child of the 1950s with the traditional television version of cowboys and Indians. His love of the outdoors made him more sympathetic to the Indians than the cowboys. He had an image in his mind that Indians were people in harmony with nature. His visit to the Rosebud was a wake-up call. White farmers controlled the lands suitable for agriculture with 100-year leases. He was shocked by the little settlements, the poverty, and the loss of the native culture. Crow Dog was trying to change all that.

After getting out of jail for his arrest at Wounded Knee II, Leonard expanded his activism. He traveled the country encouraging Native

Americans to join the American Indian Movement. Leonard was either on the phone, which was his network device or at Western Union, which was the money exchange. His wife Mary was a lovely, charismatic woman who was his partner in all this.

Qwerty wanted to join the crusade but, after returning to New York, realized that this wasn't his fight. He was glad that he could help and was hoping to talk about his feelings with Leonard.

Qwerty anxiously prepared for his visitors. He frequently looked out the window until Mary called up from a sidewalk payphone. Luckily, the young men had sleeping bags and gear. Qwerty set up Leonard, Mary and the kids in his room. After dealing with getting their van parked, he called one of his friends with benefits to arrange a sleepover. Later that evening, Qwerty and Leonard went down to the studio to talk.

"Leonard, I want to show you something."

He took out the artifacts he was studying and put them on the table. "A friend from the neighborhood gave me these one day. They are supposed to be artifacts from the Midwest found in the mounds located there. I was thinking of including them in an art project. What do you think?"

"You know the answer to that question," Leonard said, "Wait here. I'll be right back."

He returned with a canvas bag that he opened on the table. Inside was an extraordinarily beautiful peace pipe, along with some leather and feathered objects.

"After the government put my parents and grandparents on the Rosebud Reservation, soldiers came to round up anything that people had that was sacred and took their possessions away. My grandfather hid these in a hollow tree trunk. My father gave them to me. My grandfather and father were medicine men. They passed these sacred objects down to me, along with a promise never to forget the ways of our ancestors."

Qwerty felt a warm sense of just how important these objects and this struggle were. He was in awe. The pipe bowl looked like it was made of rust-colored fine-grain granite with a satin sheen.

Leonard handed him the pipe. "One day, maybe we will smoke this together."

After a long pause, he looked at Qwerty and spoke. "Try to get your sacred objects back to where they came from. They are sacred to the descendants of the ancestors who buried them. Objects can tell the story of what we do and are ordinary. Sacred objects tell the story of who we are."

"I didn't remove them, but they might have come to me for a reason. The best I can do is return them to the earth."

"In the Lakota tongue there is a greeting, *Hokahey*. Some say it is a battle cry, meaning that it is a good day to die. We won't be perfect until we die. It's OK. Maybe just returning them to earth is all you can do. Hokahey, Qwerty."

"Leonard, I wanted to ask you about something that happened when my father died. A red-tailed hawk circled in the sky above, the day we buried him."

"That was the Great Spirit sending you a sign that your father is at peace now and that you should find your own peace. He uses the hawk as a messenger. The feathers of the hawk are sacred symbols to us. It would help if you created your own symbols in your art. The spirit will let you know which ones to use if you are silent and listen."

"I am glad you came for a visit, Leonard. I admire all the work you do for your people. When I think of how my ancestors treated them, I feel ashamed."

"We live in our time, my friend. We must put one foot in front of the other and choose the right path."

When the visit was over and the group was safely on the road, Qwerty returned to sitting by his candle. He began to understand that his art and his struggle with those involved beyond the studio were equally important. The visit with Leonard reminded him that all things are connected. Qwerty didn't expect to see Leonard again. The mysterious spirit driving Leonard in his struggle was also sent to Qwerty. It was time to be silent and listen, as Leonard suggested.

When he went to his bedroom to go to sleep, a red and black quilt with the stitched figure of Crazy Horse in the middle was placed on his bed. The quilt was Mary's way of saying thank you. He wrapped the quilt around his body to feel close to them. Qwerty realized he was experiencing a connection to spiritual things greater than himself.

He had a visceral reaction when he looked at the artifacts he had discussed with Leonard. He had never believed in ghosts or feared a boogeyman in the dark, but Leonard's description of spiritual objects sent chills down his spine. He felt that Leonard's visit had a message. His art and life as an artist needed to be protected, but there were new paths to travel and new adventures to experience. The hawk was flying, and it was time to move.

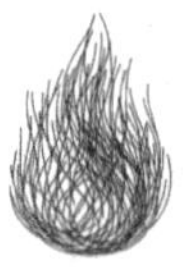

CHAPTER TWENTY

You Can't Always Get What You Want

The upper floor of Qwerty's building was nicely renovated and accessible by elevator. The light and air were refreshing, with a large skylight in the center of the space and a spiral staircase to the roof. The roof was sheltered on two sides from two taller adjacent buildings. Nomo and Qwerty had created a deck with dunnage readily available from the streets. A kiddy pool and garden hose provided all the benefits of a summer resort.

On a sunny morning, Qwerty crossed Prince Street to Dean and Delucca and bought an espresso and croissant to enjoy on the roof. Dean and Delucca was a place where he could always expect to see artists and neighbors, but this day contained a surprise. He looked up from the espresso machine and was greeted with a beautiful smile. Years ago, he first saw that smile and beautiful woman sitting at the bar at the Ocean Club. He introduced himself and got lucky. Unfortunately, she was in a serious relationship with a man away on business. She made it clear that she would stop seeing Qwerty when her boyfriend returned.

"Good to see you, Qwerty. It's been a long time. I have read a lot about your work. You must be proud."

"I suppose so. Are you still seeing your boyfriend?

"Yes, we got married. I still remember our time."

"Me too."

"Got to run, but it was nice to see you."

The affair was one of many over the years in SoHo. When he returned to the roof with his espresso, he was enjoying the pleasant memory when the phone rang. There would soon be more pressing things on his mind.

"Qwerty, it's Gunther. Are you dressed?"

"Sure, I am just having an espresso."

"Good, get two more. I am bringing over a friend from Miami."

Qwerty rushed back to Dean and Delucca to buy more espressos and treats and returned. Gunther's limo arrived on Greene Street. One of the improvements to his building was an intercom and buzzer to all floors. After entering, they took the new elevator to the penthouse floor. Qwerty's success was manifesting itself in the building upgrades.

"Qwerty this is Estefan."

"Con mucho gusto," Qwerty said.

"Igualmente, you have a beautiful place here. Is that a coffee tree under the skylight?"

"Yes, it is. I rescued it from a commercial plant store on 20th Street and 6th Avenue. The ailing tree was in the process of being rehabilitated by the owner. The guy would only sell it to me if I promised to take good care of it. I did, and it even has a few beans on it."

"Gunther, you know I made a fortune from the bushes in Columbia and exporting to the US."

Estefan and Gunther had a good laugh while Qwerty served them some espresso.

"I was telling Estefan about your going to hell piece. Do you have it set up, Qwerty?" Gunther asked.

"Sure, let's go downstairs," Qwerty said as he escorted them to the studio.

When Estefan walked into the "Go to Hell" room, he was delighted. Gunther was surprised just how much Estefan liked the work. He liked the idea of going to hell in style, and he would enjoy sharing this piece with his friends in Colombia.

"It's even better than I imagined. Could you make me an edition of five? I only brought enough money to buy one, but Gunther can handle the paperwork and delivery of the others, verdad Gunther?"

Estefan handed Qwerty a large envelope and gave him a hug.

"I see you have some pot plants upstairs. You are not very good at growing them." Estefan said while stroking his chin.

"Yeah, I think I should stick to growing tomatoes."

Estefan added, "I'll send you some seeds. They are brand new from Mexico, and you can't miss with them. Okay, Gunther, Vamonos."

After they left, Qwerty opened the envelope. It had more cash than he had ever seen at one time. He only dealt in cash with Gunther. The large amount made Qwerty wonder how much Gunther charged for his work. Qwerty was so pleased to receive a cash payment that he never bothered to check. He thought of all those parties with coke on the table. This is where all that money ends up. The best and the brightest in New York City seemed infatuated with cocaine, but few ever considered that people like Estefan were being made rich and ruining their own countries in the process. The road went on forever, and the party never ended.

Estefan and Gunther drove off in the limo on their way to dinner at the Hotel Pierre. Gunther promised to introduce Estefan to some British rock stars.

"Qwerty is a nice kid, but we may have an unpleasant business decision to make after I finalize the purchase of his career with the foundation. These artists always have the urge to keep going and make new work. Sometimes new work confuses the market, and we can't have that. They don't know when to quit. It's bad business." Gunther said as he lit a cigar and sipped scotch from the limo bar.

Estefan looked at Gunther. He snorted a line of coke from a mirrored business card. "You know, Gunther, in my line of work, I must make those types of difficult business decisions all the time. I will be happy to be of some assistance."

They laughed as the doorman at the Pierre opened the limo door.

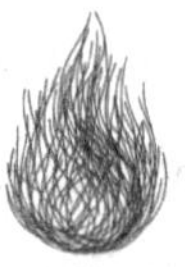

CHAPTER TWENTY-ONE

High Times at High Tide

Qwerty was busy in his Prince Street Studio preparing the copies of the video and electric devices for the "Go to Hell' piece to ship to Estefan when Gunther called.

"Qwerty, pack a bathing suit and some clothes. I want you to join me and some friends at my place in the Hamptons this weekend."

"Gunther, is Estefan going to be there? I am not comfortable around him."

"He may be around at some point; I am not sure."

Qwerty was irritated. "You know where his cash comes from, don't you?"

"Sure. Let me tell you something about cash. Cash may come with a Christmas card from your mother or from a liquor store you robbed. It is accepted wherever you want to spend it and received with a smile. Grow up, Qwerty. Do you remember that nice guy from South Africa and his family we met skiing in Zermatt? Well, he made his money supplying guns to Zimbabwe. Those guns killed a lot of innocent people. It's just business. Someone is always making too much money no matter what the economy is doing. I didn't hear you complain when he paid cash for one of your large pieces."

"Okay, I get it, Gunther."

Qwerty finished up loose ends. He felt that the situation with Gunther was getting out of control. He was thinking of Rett and a possible life together. The thought of giving up his life in New York City and starting a new life with Rett at the farm weighed on his mind.

At Michael's law office, he finalized the paperwork on the last will and testament, creating the Qwerty Blanc Foundation. He paid his bill and left some cash with Michael to be held in escrow.

He used cash to buy a new van under Hank Smith's name and registered the vehicle at the farm address. He packed the van with some of his prized possessions, including the quilt that Mary had made for him, and parked it in a parking lot on the West Side Highway. Years worth of stashing cash from Gunther's sales were stored in the farmhouse cellar. He felt the time might be right to execute a plan to leave his life as Qwerty Blanc behind. He was abandoning the life he found in SoHo. The vibrant SoHo community had vanished forever, and now it was his turn to leave.

Gunther sent a car to Prince Street Friday morning. Qwerty was approaching Gunther's beach house on Dune Road by noon. Dune Road was something that Qwerty was not accustomed to seeing.

The narrow road divided houses on the beach side that seemed big enough to be hotels and the slightly more modest houses on the bay side. Gunther's house was perched on the sand dunes with a stretch of beach as far as the eye could see. Qwerty couldn't imagine what Gunther paid for this real estate that he lived in for a few weeks in the summer. He felt that the beach should belong to everyone, not be hoarded by the rich and famous.

He was greeted at the door by Gunther's wife Uta. She was wearing a ridiculous bikini that barely contained her. Fortunately, she was draped in a silk three-quarter-length smock that blew around in the refreshing ocean breeze. She had the aura of a pole dancer past her prime.

"Quirky darling," she exclaimed, kissing him on both cheeks. He didn't bother to correct the name and returned the kisses.

"Enchante," he said, turning away and rolling his eyes.

She led him to his room to change into a bathing suit and invited him to join the group on the beach deck. He walked to the deck, where Gunther, wearing loose bathing trunks and a floppy hat, introduced him to the group.

"Everybody, this is the wonderful Qwerty Blanc. Careful he is hot you might get burned." Chuckles all around. "Qwerty, I would like to introduce Philippa and Heiner."

He introduced him to several other guests he had seen before at galleries. He couldn't remember whether they were from Pace, Marlborough, or other midtown venues.

They enjoyed that sunny afternoon on the beach, drinking, chatting, and running in and out of the waves. The atmosphere was festive, and it was easy to forget the world while basking on the beach and absorbing the ocean mist.

Later in the afternoon, Qwerty wandered about the house while Gunther, Uta, and some of the guests took a jaunt in Gunther's motorboat out in Shinnecock Bay. Qwerty found himself in Gunther's study, noticing ledgers and notebooks scattered across the credenza and desk. He couldn't resist reading through the material. There were binders with artists' names that he was quite familiar with, including one with his name on it.

The binders were neatly organized and filled with notes and dates as well as strategies for affecting the market prices. The catalogs, photos, and ledgers were carefully arranged by date, starting with the earliest to the present. The ledgers were divided into two groups. One showed actual gallery and auction sales. The other ledger had different dollar amounts with columns listing transactions between Gunther and members of his group. In some early transactions, the balances were wildly negative, but as time went on, the ratio reversed. It appeared that the group was buying the artworks bought at auctions and galleries at progressively inflated prices to establish these prices in the marketplace. Once these inflated prices were established, they would cash in. Gunther recorded the exhibits and records of legitimate sales methodically. The notes were a giddy set of notations on the strategy to inflate the prices and further the fame of their artists.

After reading his own file, Qwerty realized that the dealers who had helped him initially were out of the picture and not included in the process. Richard and Leo were not part of Gunther's group or scheme. They were useless to Gunther except for finding and developing real talent and getting them started. He recalled overhearing Gunther on the telephone with a dealer in Milan named Luciano. He was discussing a Rauschenberg painting that Leo had sent to Italy. Leo was asking $60,000.00 for the painting. Gunther told Luciano to buy it. Gunther noted that the next step was to get the painting at a major auction to overbid the price and resell the painting. He also noted that Leo was too old-fashioned and didn't understand how they were turning the market. He also noted that serious investors could drive blue chip prices into the millions.

When Qwerty was reading his binder, he realized that Gunther had bought the rights to many of his early and current works. The notes indicated that his works didn't fit the market for his blue-chip artist scheme and that he needed other strategies to raise the price.

It made perfect sense to pass Qwerty to the DIA Foundation, which was outside the scheme, meant well, and guaranteed long-term fame and value for an artist's career. The DIA Foundation had a good track record of showcasing artists' works and supporting the artists they signed. The part that Qwerty was not prepared to accept was how an artist could relinquish creative control once the foundation assumed control of public access to the work.

Qwerty walked along the beach with the rhythm of the waves rolling onto the shore and the cool, damp sand between his toes, remembering the joy of discovery with each artwork he created. He remembered how much fun it was collaborating with Nomo and how he had been given a gift that young Hank Smith had never dreamed of achieving or using. Looking back, he remembered the excitement of the early candle works at the pop-up shows. He remembered the excitement of his first show with "Fire and Rain." Every piece had that moment in the studio when the idea became a reality, and he could sit back and marvel at the process. There were times when he felt that he had joined the ancient masters of art.

He was now being asked to give all that up by accepting the terms of a DIA contract. He traded financial security and career management in exchange for never truly creating art again. He would be allowed to replicate himself but not to reinvent himself. He thought of Rett and the farm. His return to being Hank Smith again didn't require reinventing himself. He simply had to let Qwerty die and leave him behind for the system to idolize and for the foundation to glorify. Hank Smith would not exist for them.

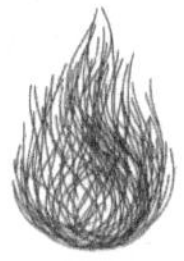

Chapter Twenty-Two

We Got to Get Out of this Place If It's the Last Thing We Ever Do.

The evening was glorious as only an ocean beach could offer in late summer. Qwerty had learned to dress the part of a New York artist and came down to the dining room with baggy tan pants, a floppy blue blazer, a tank top, and a scarf around his neck. No one could accuse him of not looking the part. The large white room had a grand piano at one end. Couches and loveseats were covered loosely with white cotton fabric, facing the terrace and the majestic Atlantic Ocean. To the right was another grouping of sofas facing the ocean and a wood pellet stove fireplace. At the end of the grand room was a long dining table with a raised ceiling with a skylight and chandelier over the table. Qwerty imagined how many famous artists, titans of finance, and important political types had sat at that table and listened to a rock star play the piano after dinner.

"Ah! There is our red-hot artist." Gunther said as Qwerty entered the space.

Gunther's guests included a few more unfamiliar faces. The ambient sound of chatting and pleasant music was in the air. Servers passed around tasty little snacks. All the guests seemed to be in a good mood. The beachwear uniform of the day had changed into sleek, sexy outfits and lots of sparkle from the lady's jewelry.

Gunther walked Qwerty over to Heinrich, who greeted him with, "So this is the young man who will be joining our DIA family. We are so pleased."

Qwerty smiled but felt a knot in his stomach at the thought of giving his creative life to others.

"Pardon us a second," Gunther told Heinrich as he escorted Qwerty to his den.

"Just a formality, but you need to sign these documents for the foundation," handing Qwerty a folder of papers.

Qwerty looked at Gunther and asked," Does this release me from our verbal contract?"

"Yes, of course, you belong to the foundation now."

Qwerty heard the words and imagined he might as well be one of Gunther's thoroughbred horses being put out to stud. At least he would no longer be part of the scheme that Gunther and his group had put together. He remembered the day that Nomo was unceremoniously dumped. Fortunately for Nomo, there was an alternative. Gunther dropped Alan's painting career after being told there wasn't room for another painter focused on all-white canvasses. Alan's career floundered and he had a heart attack after a night of drinking and snorting coke. No one seemed to care or link the two issues, and few attended his funeral. His girlfriend took over his loft and rolled up the canvasses.

Qwerty didn't have an issue with the foundation, but he was uneasy about the system of buying and selling creative careers. Something just didn't pass the smell test.

Dinner was pleasant, and some Wiener Schnitzels were in honor of Gunther's German heritage. After dessert, everyone sat around the cloth-covered sofas drinking, and there were lines of coke on the glass-topped tables. Qwerty slipped away before the coke brought on a middle-aged orgy.

Qwerty knew he was an outlier in this gathering. He wanted no part of the future laid out for him. Making art was frustrating at times but was as natural as breathing. These people took the oxygen from the air. He needed the fresh air of his past. He longed for the river of his childhood home that flowed by and through him, the sights and sounds of the old farmland and the constantly changing local weather. He also thought of Rett and his growing love for her.

Sleep didn't come easy that night. In the morning, he strolled the beach. The guests scattered around, visiting other friends nearby.

Gunther offered Qwerty the use of his boat to take out on Shinnecock Bay. Gunther thought he might enjoy that and offered to drop him off at the Marina. Qwerty was suspicious that this offer had strings attached. Perhaps poor Qwerty might drown because he was not a good swimmer.

The time was right to get away permanently and disappear. He loved being an artist, but the world he had entered in his early days was gone. Artists who had once explored the Bowery were now exploring real estate in the Hamptons. Champions of American Art were joining forces with Wall Street financiers in conspicuous consumption. Qwerty's world was fading and Hank's world was calling to him. It was time for action.

Qwerty changed into his bathing suit and packed his small bag with some clothes. He went into the den. He quietly gathered Gunther's folders from the credenza and packed them in his case with a plastic bag.

Gunther waved from the garage in his red jeep. "Ready for a nice outing in the boat."

"Thank you, Gunther. I need a getaway."

Gunther showed Qwerty to his boat and waved goodbye. "Careful out there. The currents are treacherous."

"Not as treacherous as you," Qwerty said quietly, smiling and waving from the boat.

The afternoon sun sparkled on the surface of the bay with a breeze that filled his lungs with exhilarating coolness. He heard freedom calling as he headed out to the middle of the bay.

He stopped the engine and let the boat drift and took off his clothes to lie naked in the sunshine. Gunther had left a well-stocked bar, so he took a bottle of Makers Mark bourbon and drank freely from the bottle. After basking in the sun, he fell asleep on the deck.

Qwerty awoke as the late afternoon sunshine went down on the horizon. The boat had drifted near the inlet, with the stone jetty in sight. He took one more drink of Makers Mark bourbon.

His plan was clear, and his heart began to pound in his chest. He poured gasoline around the boat. He then went down into the galley to find a cleaver and returned to the deck.

In the distance, he saw a motorboat traveling out of the marina where Gunther had kept his boat. The approaching motorboat in the distance set the timing. He had a small backpack with clothes and his wallet. He stripped down and placed his hand on the bathing suit and tee shirt set on the deck of the boat. With one violent blow of the cleaver, he severed the end of his pinky finger. Blood spurted out of the end of his finger onto his bathing suit and tee shirt. His hand became numb. The sensation was painful, but that soon passed, being replaced by a sense of complete freedom from pleasing people at the expense of his principles. He wrapped the end of his severed finger in the blood-soaked bathing suit and shirt. He carefully placed his fingertip and bloody clothes in a life preserver so that they would be found as evidence of his demise. His bag was ready to toss overboard for the swim back to Southampton. All that remained was to place Gunther's folders and ledgers in the plastic bag and set them afloat. He thought the authorities might find the contents of the paperwork interesting. Gunther would have some explaining to do.

He spread more gasoline around the boat and climbed down the side of the boat with his bag. With a flick of his cigarette lighter, the boat burst into flames as he slipped away, quietly swimming into the gentle water of Shinnecock Bay. The mysterious boat that had left the Marina suddenly came about and returned to the Marina. The fire and police would soon arrive. The artist who started his career with a candle had gone into history in a burst of flames. This would be a fitting end.

The water in the bay enveloped him. There were swimmers in the evening sun at the beach at the inlet on the South Hampton side. He knew he could blend in and disappear. As he walked along the beach, he could see Gunther's boat in flames drifting on the bay and hear the sound of sirens. The image of himself as the famous Qwerty Blanc drifted slowly toward the bottom of the bay like a flat stone that once skipped along the surface. Qwerty was dead. Long live Hank Smith.

When he reached shore, he changed into his clothes and walked to the train station. The last train to New York City was late but on its way. The next stop after the train ride would be his van parked in the lot on the West Side Highway. Tears filled his eyes as he reached for a pay phone and dialed.

"Rett? I needed to hear your voice. I am heading home and to you."

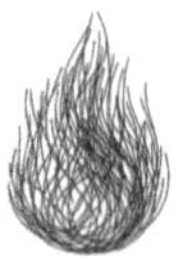

CHAPTER TWENTY-THREE

The Long Road Home

September in the lower Adirondack Mountains is a time to enjoy the summer's serene memories and prepare for the long, solemn winter. The light changes in late August from the glow of the growing season to a clear, piercing light that signals temperature swings and the time to harvest. The old timers say there is a specific day that the light changes. They say the livestock start to grow their winter coats and the weeds begin to die. Only those blessed with a keen sensitivity to nature are aware of that day. By September, there is no doubt for anyone that the light had changed and was bringing on the Fall season.

The new millennium had just begun. The Smith farm on the banks of the Battenkill hadn't changed much since the days when Alice Smith and Adam Deedle raised Hank there. The corn fields were now hay fields and the wooded pastures and wetlands had replaced the pastures on the steep hills and valleys. Thanks to conservation efforts, eagles and wild turkeys returned in large numbers. The farmhouse now produced the sounds of a family and a school bus stopped on the nearby town road on weekdays.

Rett had completed her master's degree in environmental studies at Cornell University long ago and was now working for the New York State Department of Environmental Conservation. Hank had wasted no time after disappearing from his life as Qwerty Blanc in New York City to win her love and propose marriage. They were married in a ceremony at the farm, and settled into married life. Rett gave birth to a boy and a girl. Both children were good-looking, creative, and inquisitive. Hank named their boy Jackson after Jackson Pollack. Rett named their daughter Summer because she wanted her to have a life of sunshine.

From time to time, Hank would reflect on his life in SoHo and his career. There were even times when he missed the energy and passion that he experienced in his studio. At those times, he realized that the chapter of Qwerty's story had a beginning, a middle, and an end. It was an important chapter in his life, but only a chapter.

As time passed, he began to see his life in total and that all the pieces were blessed. The sunshine and the beauty of the early fall warmed his skin and the smell of a distant woodfire added seasoning to the fresh breeze that filled his lungs. He climbed down from his tractor and returned to his house to greet his children. Both were instilled with a love of the outdoors and a respect for nature. Jackson was especially fond of tying flies from wild bird feathers for trout fishing.

Jackson proudly displayed a trout fly that he had created and said, "I hope you think my fly is beautiful."

"Jack, when you are tying this fly, you are imitating a real mayfly or some other critter from the river. Your audience is made up of trout. The trout will tell you that it is beautiful by jumping for it. That is your measure of success."

"But Dad, I want it to look beautiful so that people can see what a beautiful thing I have made."

"You are making beautiful things. It doesn't matter what people think, son. Some people appreciate its beauty, and others don't, but the trout will always tell you the truth."

Hank said, "Okay. Enough lectures, let's grab our flyrods and try out some of your flies on the river."

Summer was a child with her own unique view of life. Her intelligence and curiosity attracted people and brought them into whatever she was doing. Hank stayed back and gave her room just to be herself. He enjoyed the entire process.

When Summer saw Hank and Jack with their flyrods, she called, "Hey, wait for me!"

Usually, after catching trout, they would let them go back into the river, but this time, they decided to surprise Rett with a fried fish dinner when she returned from work. When Rett came home, the dining room table and lighted candles were set.

"What a nice surprise. Is that fried trout?" Rett said with tears in her eyes.

"We made apple pie for dessert. I remember Adam saying: it's a shame to let them apples go to waste." Hank added, "Let's eat!"

When everyone was settling in for the night, Rett turned to Hank and asked, "Do you ever miss your old life in New York City?"

"No, just all those pretty girls."

That started a pillow fight.

The following Sunday morning, the family was gathered on the deck overlooking the river. There were the sounds of birds and the breeze filtering through the trees. The Sunday New York Times was delivered by mail once a week by special arrangement. The headline in the Art section was entitled, "Qwerty Blanc Laser Earthwork Celebrates the Equinox." The article described the giant laser light show at the North and South Pole. The installation was photographed via satellite. The work was done posthumously based on the concept of the late artist Qwerty Blanc with funds provided by the DIA Foundation and the Qwerty Blanc Foundation with special assistance from NASA.

In another section, there was an article about Gunther Reinhardt being released from jail on probation. The article described how Gunther was found guilty of tax evasion in connection with his art dealings. The article mentioned the mysterious death of the artist Qwerty Blanc and the discovery of documents leading to Gunther's arrest.

Summer had the Art section in hand and was reading the latest reviews. "I want to be an artist when I grow up," Summer proclaimed.

"Your future is yours for the taking, sweetheart," her mother replied. "Is there anything interesting this week?"

"There is this crazy article about some art spectacle at the North and South Pole."

"That is fascinating, honey."

"Hmm," Hank said, clearing his throat.

After breakfast, the family set out for the day's activities in a field below the farmhouse. Hank was driving his old Ford 800 tractor. Jackson Smith was carrying a fly rod waving to him as he walked across the field toward the Battenkill. Summer Smith was running behind Jackson in her bathing suit and carrying a sketch pad. Looking up from planting a small tree on the bank of the river was Rett.

A Red-Tailed Hawk circled above them in the clear blue sky.

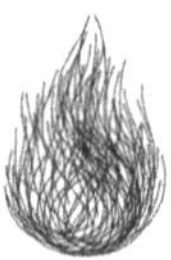

The End